The Deadlands Epitaph

Volume 1, Issue 2

Editor-in-Chief: John Goff
Graphic Design: Zeke Sparkes, Chris Libey, John Hopler, Chuck Croft
Pinnacle Staff: Mario Lee Bansen III, Michelle Hensley, Dave Wilson, Allen Seyberth

Contents

The Big Picture

Howdy and welcome back to the second issue of the *Epitaph*!

If you're unfamiliar with our *Hell on Earth* setting, check out the full-color comic in the back, by veteran writing team Clay and Susan Griffith and drawn by one of our most popular artists, Richard Pollard. It features Gabriel Roth, his twin pistols, a whole passel of targets, and an old friend—or maybe foe!

We've also included another bit of prime salvage for our Wasted West fans—a *Hell on Earth* adventure by Jay Kyle, who's life's ambition is to become a post-Apocalyptic warlord. It spotlights the abominations dearest to our hearts here at Pinnacle: good, old walkin' dead. But lest you experienced wasters scoff, the zombies are liable to get a little payback in *Biodome 2*!

Our latest piece of fiction by *Deadlands* trail boss John Goff tells the tale of Ronan Lynch and proves that a little knowledge isn't always such a good thing. Join him as he begins to uncover the true secrets of the *Weird West*!

You'll also find the first installments of several regular columns, including *The Armory*, *Varmints!*, and several others.

This month's *Armory* piece, named *The Guns o' the South*, gives your Confederate gunslingers a few choices for hoglegs besides those confounded Yankee-made smokewagons. This article is just the thing to flesh out your favorite Texas Ranger.

Varmints! contains an abomination that's traveled half-way around the globe to make it into this issue, the spirit 'glom, a submission by our favorite Kiwi, Brian Leybourne. Backing up the new horror is an old one that snuck out of the pages of *Rascals, Varmints, & Critters II: The Book of Curses*.

We've got a few mistakes and misprints to correct and clarify in our *Gremlins* section. We'll be posting these to our website as well, but since not everybody has access to high-falutin' stuff like the Internet we thought we should put them in here too!

And that's not all that's hiding in this issue either, but it should get your mouth watering!

But first, it's time to catch our compadres up on what's been happening out there in the Weird and Wasted West. Kicking off this shindig are setting updates for both *Deadlands* and *Hell on Earth* by the respective brand mangers: John Goff and John Hopler.

WEIRD WEST ROUNDUP

Since last issue, a whole stampede of trouble has broke loose in the Weird West. As usual, the best place to get the story is from Lacey O'Malley down Tombstone way, even if the viewpoint is a little slanted!

THE CALIFORNIA FREE STATE?

For the better part of 15 years, the Union and Confederacy have been fighting over California, with Mexcio occasionally slipping in a sucker-punch or two. That doesn't even include the recent declaration of sovereignty by Reverend Grimme's Lost Angels or the numerous petty "warlords" who've staked out a claim in the ruins of the Maze. Well, it looks like the leveler heads out on the coast have finally had enough!

Over the past few months, politically-minded folks in the Maze have been promoting a democratic solution to the Golden State's dilemma. To resolve the issue, a referendum is being held soon in Sacramento, the state's capital.

Although the Confederacy has its supporters in the upcoming vote, the safe money is between the Union, which claims the lion's share of the state, or complete independence of the sort practiced by Utah, a.k.a. Deseret.

While many settled folks are partial to Union-leanings, observers shouldn't underestimate the number of free-spirits drawn to the Maze by the lure of easy money. It's possible these saddletramps may throw their weight behind a free California.

Insiders report that the Independence Movement, as it's calling itself, seems to have at least one powerful financial backer who's not yet revealed himself. According to the local rumor mill, this shadow behind the throne may be anyone from the northern rail baron Kang to the eccentric Emperor Norton to Reverend Grimme to Santa Anna himself.

This reporter finds all of those choices ironic, as they are the very reason for the push for a settlement! That news may darkly foreshadow the Maze's fate should Independence win the day.

BAYOU VERMILLION THUGS FAR AND WIDE

If you remember, we reported last issue on the possible dire straits of the Bayou Vermillion Railroad's financial status. Our sources across the West have since noticed agents of the BV making appearances in regions outside the railroad's usual area of operations.

LaCroix's envoys have been spotted from eastern Kentucky all the way to central California. There are reports of BV representatives in Mississippi as well, certainly closer to the railroad's home of New Orleans, but nonetheless outside its normal routes—unless whispers about a buyout or partnership with the Kansas City & Little Rock rail company are true.

Even those regions aren't truly that surprising, however, given the Bayou Vermillion's ambitions of securing a trans-continental contract with the Confederate government. What is unexpected are unconfirmed visits by LaCroix's agents near Salt Lake City and Provo in Deseret and even crossing the border into the Yankee Northeast!

Exactly what purpose these far-flung excursions serve is unclear, although most foks in the know figure they tie in with "Baron" LaCroix's unsubstantiated monetary problems. This reporter has a nagging suspicion that there's more to the field trips than meets the eye—or accountant.

As always, you can count on the *Epitaph* to keep you infomed!

RUMBLINGS FROM THE SOUTH

If Bayou Vermillion's shenanigans weren't enough to keep eyes on the Southwest in fear of a renewed flare-up of the "Rail Wars," it looks like our one-legged friend from south of the border may be getting fiesty again.

If you'll remember last year, the "good" Reverend Grimme issued his Edict of 1877, declaring the City of Lost Angels and an area 75 miles around it to be an independent sovereign state. The Confederate government, not needing *another* target at which to point its guns, has steered clear of the area—so far.

With the absence of a strong military presence and the rich veins of ghost rock tempting both Emperor Maximillian and his French puppet masters, it really was only a matter of time before Mexico made more aggressive "offers" on Californian real estate. It looks like time is quickly running out for the Maze, if not other areas of the Southwest.

Numerous reports have filtered into the offices here in Tombstone indicating the massing of forces on the Mexican border. Santa Anna may have been hoping for a surprise rush across the border, because word has it that much of the troop movements are taking place at night.

Who knows what this means for the upcoming Californian elections? Reverend Grimme may find himself in need of mending fences with the Confederacy. He and his "church" may talk tough, but this reporter doubts they're a match for a seasoned plunderer like Santa Anna!

Gold Found in Alaska Territory!

It appears that U.S. Secretary of State, William Seward, wasn't as foolish as most citizens of the Union thought in purchasing the Alaska Territory from Russia. Rumors have filtered down from the Washington Territory that prospectors are claiming to have found massive gold strikes there.

Already, the Union's northwestern ports of Tacoma and Seattle are feeling an increase as miners begin filtering to the Great White North in search of fortune. It wouldn't surprise this reporter to learn no small number of former Confederates are filtering north to grab a few claims of their own. No doubt, profiteers will soon be gouging prices in the distant territory.

As an interesting complication, some of our sources are of the opinion that the strikes were actually found on *Canadian* soil. Given the current state of affairs betweeen the Union and Canada, this should make for some interesting times up there if nothing else!

"Unusual" Cattle Spells Success for

Morgan Cattle Company!

The Morgan Cattle Company of Ghost Creek, California has recently gained some notoriety among finer dining establishments back East. Their hybrid Angus beef is being lauded as the top choice among many of the poshest restaurants on both sides of the Mason-Dixon.

Scientists at the nearby Distinguished Collegium of Interspacial Physics in Gomorra have taken an interest in the apparently new breed of cattle—and they're not the only ones looking toward Ghost Creek. It seems the town is well named, as a massive ghost rock strike has just been discovered under the water table in the region. This new lode has caught the attention of a few other Gomorra residents as well, namely the Sweetrock Mining Company.

What this means for Morgan Cattle Company, long used to free range grazing, has yet to be seen...

High Tales of Hell on Earth

Let's take a look at some of the happenings throughout the Wasted West.

Mystery Explosions

The survivors of a scattered Combine tribute caravan have been spreading stories about some mysterious explosions that destroyed a Black Hat outpost in southwestern Colorado.

According to the caravan members, their convoy was approaching the small fort the Combine had established to collect tribute when it was suddenly rocked by a number of large explosions followed by a series of small blasts that sounded like a string of firecrackers going off. "There was a bunch of sparkling explosions like fireworks," said one dazed survivor, "then the whole thing disappeared in a cloud of dust and smoke."

Most of the fort's garrison were killed or wounded by the explosions; the survivors were finished off by the members of the caravan, who then fled west. Some of the convoy members reported a loud wailing noise just before the explosions, suggesting that they may have been the result of some sort of artillery attack.

DEATH IN TRANSYLVANIA

The undead have come to Transylvania—Transylvania, Louisiana, that is. This small survivor community on the west bank of the Mississippi was overrun by a horde of walkin' dead that emerged from the river. The dripping dead tore through the small town in a matter of minutes, leaving few survivors. Once the killer corpses had ravaged the town, they disappeared back beneath the waters of the Ol' Muddy.

This attack has prompted the River Watch to step up its patrols in the area, but no evidence of the undead horde or reasons for the attack have surfaced (like the walkin' dead need a reason).

CROAKER ATTACKS ON THE RISE

Something seems to have put a bee in the croaker's collective bonnet. Miners and traders throughout the central Maze have reported an increasing number of attacks by croakers. One of the local Law Dogs, Angus McPherson reports that he has come across at least five derelict craft on his patrols in the area. All of these boats were found adrift without any crew aboard. There were no bodies, but plenty of signs of a struggle: bloodstains, empty shell casings, broken equipment, etc.

Croakers have always been a hazard in the area, but no one can remember this many attacks in such a short period of time. McPherson has taken up a collection from many of the local survivor communities and is using the trade goods to hire a posse. He plans to step up patrols in the area, and if he can recruit enough bodies, he hopes to provide escorts to traders.

NEXT ISSUE

Next issues brings you a brand new 14 page comic and a brand new adventure. Of course, that's nowhere near all! We'll have more of our regular monthly installments (like the *Armory* and *Varmints!*), some inside info on *Lost Colony*, and—just because it fits the theme of the *Epitaph*—the scoop on journalists in the *Weird West*!

SUBMISSIONS

As we mentioned last issue, the *Epitaph* is a great place to get your ideas, stories, or adventures for the *Deadlands* settings published by us. Our sourcebooks are kept pretty close to our vest, but the *Eptiaph* gives us the opportunity to let our fans show off their own talent. And who knows? An article in this quarterly might be the stepping stone to even more opportunities down the trail!

Since we're trying to pack this book with as much material for our games as we possibly can, we're going to be partial to shorter articles—say 1000 to 3000 words. Adventures probably need to go a bit above that count, into the 8000 to 10000 word range. More than that, though, and the piece is taking a sizeable chunk of the *Epitaph*. If it is the coolest thing since the Clockwork De-Moler, we might can be convinced to accept a longer piece, but don't mortgage the ranch on it!

We prefer paper submissions mailed to our address below. Don't forget to include a signed copy of the evaluation waiver on our website; we can't even glance at your piece without it.

Pinnacle Entertainment Group, Inc.
P.O. Box 10908
Blacksburg, VA 24062-0908

Webpage (for waiver); www.peginc.com

Email questions/comments to:
Deadlands@deadlands.com

BIODOME 2

AN ADVENTURE FOR DEADLANDS: HELL ON EARTH

So, Marshal, you say you're posse is too tough for good, old-fashioned, walkin' dead. Well, have we got an adventure for you!

The Story So Far...

In the final years of the twentieth century, an ambitious ecological project called Biosphere2 was undertaken in the desert near the small town of Oracle, Arizona. B2, as it was commonly known, was a 7.2 million cubic-foot, sealed glass and spaceframe structure, and was touted by the Confederate government as a way of testing the feasibility of long-term human habitation within a sealed environment.

Construction began in 1988, and cost over $150 million to build the 3.15 acre apparatus. Inside the facility were seven wilderness ecosystems, including a rainforest and a 900,000-gallon ocean and a human habitat.

The system had an unprecedented capacity for sensing and controlling its internal environment. Seven hundred fifty sensors monitored the vital statistics of this living laboratory—measuring temperature, light, humidity, carbon dioxide and other qualities of the air and soil. In response to these readings, operators could, for example, turn on blowers for cooling and heating or create a miniature rainstorm to change the humidity. B2's own nuclear, and later ghost-rock, reactor provided the power.

All Is Not Well

The first crew—four women and four men—entered Biosphere2 on September 26, 1991. The claimed objective of the experiment was to assess the operations of the technical and biological systems. The crew remained inside for two years despite the mysterious deaths of three members. They finally emerged on September 26, 1993.

After a six-month transition period, a second crew of seven (this time five men and two women) entered B2. They remained inside for six and a half months before four more deaths occurred. The survivors were immediately released on September 17, 1994.

Of these fortunate escapees, two were admitted to a private psychiatric institute for readjustment to a normal life. The other survivor disappeared only to show up six months later at the offices of the *Tombstone Epitaph,* where she claimed that B2 was a huge cover story for a sinister project designed to experiment on human guinea pigs. An investigation by the Texas Rangers was inconclusive. Shortly thereafter, a fire at the hospital-institute where the other two crewmembers were recovering claimed 36 lives, including the two survivors.

The project seemed cursed and was abandoned.

Biosphere2 was turned over to the University of Arizona, which used it as a research and educational center for advanced research in the fields of ecology and agricultural advancement. The center became a popular tourist attraction for those who heard stories of the "insane astronauts" and "murderous isolationists", as well as conspiracy nuts who believed that the Texas Rangers didn't release all of their findings. The small town of Oracle prospered from the increased tourism well into the next century.

The GAIA Project

Around 2040, the Biosphere2 center was purchased from the University of Arizona by an agricultural research corporation called Gersholm Industries and was renamed the GAIA project at Oracle (Gersholm Agricultural Industrial Advancement). While rumors abounded that Gersholm Industries was somehow connected to Hellstromme, the claims were never proven.

Gersholm Industries bought out Oracle's residents and businesses for an exorbitant sum and forced them to move. The company increased security around the site, leveling Oracle in the process. Within the next five years, the town was little but a memory.

Tourists who still flocked to see the B2 "massacre" site were turned away, and as the years passed, even the die-hard conspiracy nuts found other places to go. For the next 35 years, the complex sat in the hills of Arizona in secrecy and relative security. Whatever went on behind its tall fences and sealed doors was unknown to the public at large.

During the Last War, LatAm forces bypassed the area in their drive for the Pinal Pass to the north and subsequent retreat back to the border. The GAIA Project was spared the onslaught of the ghost rock bombs, as Oracle wasn't close to any military targets. By Judgment Day the only people who even remembered it existed were a handful of locals and a few conspiracy theorists and/or nuts.

When things started to quiet down after the war, the GAIA Project made itself known again. Dr. Hans Aubrecht Gersholm, founder of the project, began to carefully and quietly trade with nearby survivor communities. What they had to offer was nothing short of amazing: fruits, vegetables, and grains of incredible quality and size.

Biofear, Too

The truth about Biosphere2 is as sinister as the theorists claimed.

Its original purpose was an arena where hapless victims could be psychologically tortured without outside interference to generate concentrated terror. Hidden among the various atmospheric, soil, and temperature sensors were highly sophisticated empathic detectors that allowed the team's emotional responses to be monitored and evaluated. In effect, it was an attempt to understand how the events of the Reckoning fed on fear.

However, it proved too much for the government researchers to handle. None of the crewmembers were told of the true nature of the experiment, so when the emotional pressure reached the breaking point, the situation got out of control. After the second crew's

Biodome2

early and catastrophic failure, backing for the project wavered. The public exposure—even in a questionable rag like the *Epitaph*—was the final nail in the coffin; the government pulled the plug and eliminated all witnesses it could lay its hands on.

Gersholm Agricultural Industrial Advancement, a subsidiary of Hellstromme Industries, got wind of the true nature of B2, and leapt at the opportunities it presented. The GAIA project used the tremendous array of sensors to turn B2 into a sort of scaled fear "super-conductor" along the lines of Hellstromme's first ghost-steel rail line/roundhouse experiments (as detailed in *The Marshal's Handbook* and the *City o' Gloom* for *Deadlands: the Weird West*).

This unique environment also provided fertile ground for Gersholm's experiments in the applications of manitou harnessing. The good doctor developed a variety of ways to use modified spirit fetters, and fired up a large antenna, the Manitou Capacitor Array, which is designed to draw even more spiritual energy into B2. This spritual energy is then used in another of the good Doctor's creations: the Tethered Organic Fertilization Unit (TOFU). This is a modified spirit fetter that provides a sort of "super-fertilizer" to the gardens of B2.

This latter function continues today, and has become even more effective since the end of the world.

The MCA

The Manitou Capacitor Array functions as a huge spirit magnet, attracting manitous from the surrounding area to B2 like flies to a corpse. Once drawn, the MCA can trap and store up to six manitous at a time in a special shielded containment unit. Gersholm then hooks a TOFU implanted host body up to the MCA and forcibly inters a manitou into it. After removing the head, Gersholm has a rather grotesque "spirit battery" with which to fertilize his crops.

The MCA cannot pull a manitou from a host body, but the attraction effect nonetheless draws a manitou (and its host, if there is one) towards the array.

The Setup

The posse is passing through Arizona when they wander into the small town of Globe. The village is suffering from an affliction all too common in the Wasted West—famine. A mutant strain of weevils has wiped out the entire scraggly crop of foodstuffs the survivors had managed to eek out of the harsh Southwestern soil.

The leader of the community, a middle-aged woman named Rebecca Bradford, approaches the posse and asks for its help—particularly if it includes any obvious do-gooders like heretic Doomsayers or Law Dogs. She's heard tell of the GAIA project from passing traders and wants to establish trade with it if at all possible. To that end, they recently sent a trade caravan out with the majority of the town's valuables in the hope of securing food.

That was nearly two weeks ago.

Chapter One: Hitting the Road

Now, she's worried something terrible has befallen the townsfolk that went; if so, not only are they in danger, but the whole town may starve! She asks the heroes to head toward GAIA to find out what happened, and, if possible, arrange for foodstuffs as well. Globe's short on food, but near enough to Phoenix (and hungry enough) to chance a few raids into the battlefields for valuable salvage, if that's what it takes.

Bradford doesn't have a lot to offer the posse for their help besides the warm-and-fuzzy feeling of a job well done, but the townsfolk can scrounge a few odds and ends. Feel free to make the offer suit your campaign, Marshal.

Assuming the posse accepts Bradford's offer (and they must have, else you wouldn't be reading this, Marshal), she gives them directions to the GAIA project. It lies about four days drive or eight days foot-march from Globe. Cutting due south through the mountains is slow going, since the highway department just isn't what it used to be.

The route skirts the edges of the Phoenix battlefield and, although the way is risky, she suspects her traders took that one as time is of the essence. She asks the heroes to follow the same route and provides them with a rough map. Bradford ends by advising them to steer clear of actually entering the battlefield, though, because brain-hungry walkin' dead toting assault rifles are the least of the dangers there.

Less than a day's drive (two days' walk) from Globe, the posse finds what's left of the trade caravan. We're jumping right into the action here, so get things moving as fast as possible. The party must deal with a literal legion of undead later on, so play this encounter tough and hard. Make them respect the power of the zombies so that when they're confronted by hundreds of them, they'll know to run instead of trying to fight every single one.

The Last (Vegetable) Stand

The action starts as the heroes are whizzing down the highway (or trekking across the wastes). They see a small band of humans atop an overturned tractor-trailer surrounded by a few other smoking wrecks and a small horde of undead. A waist-high pile of vegetables has spilled from the back of the trailer and is quickly rotting in the hot Arizona sun.

As the heroes get closer, they see scores of zombies have already been put down. The three survivors atop the rig seem low on ammo, and are saving their shots only for the few horrors that try to climb up to their perch. On a Hard (9) Cognition roll, the posse might also notice that the spoiling veggies are much larger than usual.

Now it's time to play hero. There are 3 zombies for every character in the group, plus a few more if you feel the need to make 'em waste some ammo. Use the stats for regular walkin' dead from the Hell on Earth rulebook. None of these brain-eaters have weapons (other than bones or crowbars). If your posse is particularly tough, Marshal, you can use veteran walkin' dead instead and give them a few firearms.

A smart posse doesn't have to fight them all—it could lead them away with a clever distraction as well.

After the fight (or rescue), allow the heroes to introduce themselves and their mission. The survivors then tell the heroes their tale of woe.

"My name's Jose. Me and my crew were supposed to drive this truck down to Oracle. Ever heard of the GAIA Project? Some scientist has been growing produce there for a few years now. These super-vegetables are new (Jose picks up a 5 pound tomato and takes a bite out of it). Doc Gersholm—that's the scientist—says these'll feed the whole West." "Shoulda figured it was too good to be true."

"We see things on this highway all the time, but I ain't never run into so many stinkin' deaders. We tried to plow through but they just got stuck in the wheels and caused me to wreck. I told the rest of the caravan to leave us but they wouldn't hear of it. So they got wiped out as well."

"We'da died up there if it hadn't been for you."

After the heroes ask whatever other questions they have, Jose throws them one last curveball.

"Look, I know I ain't got no right to ask you this, but all these zombies—they weren't the only ones we saw. We passed two other swarms—big ones—heading south. Right up toward Oracle.

"I got a bad feeling they don't want this produce gettin' out to folks. Like Rebecca told you,

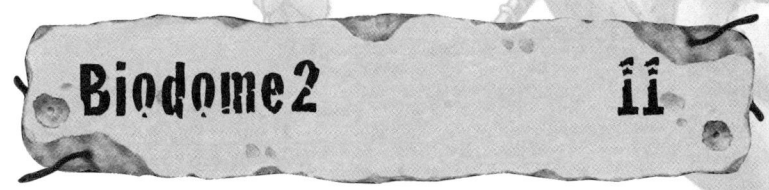

we're real short on food and are going to have to work for weeks to scrounge enough to get another load of veggies like this— if GAIA even survives."

"Somebody needs to go up there, take a look, and maybe pull those folks' fat out of the fire. We're about out of ammo—and we're sure out of folks to shoot it after this mess. We can't offer you anything beyond what Rebecca already ponied up, but if there is trouble, Doc Gersholm's gonna be a rich man soon. I'm sure he'd pay well to have people like yourselves on his team."

Off to Oracle

Outskirts of Phoenix Battlefields, AZ, Fear Level 4

The posse's trip south of Globe down old Arizona Route 77 is scenic and uneventful. The highway is in poor condition, but many of the wrecks have been pushed off onto the shoulder. As the posse climbs into Pinal Pass, however, they find the remains of a major battlefield. The burned-out, rusted hulks of Conquistador Main Battle Tanks and Matador APCs lie alongside M-10 Lee MBTs and Stuart APCs.

The wrecks been picked clean over the years, but an Incredible (11) *scroungin'* roll turns up one useful weapon in an overturned Matador: a M-200 Man Portable Support Weapon (detailed in *The Wasted West* sourcebook). The weapon has only the normal heavy bipod. It also has a partial belt of 26 rounds of 20mm ammunition.

Artillery strikes have turned the landscape into a bizarre imitation of a moonscape. Aircraft and helicopter wreckage attests to the ferocity of the combat, but no bodies are found.

Anyone venturing off either side of the road runs into a density 5 field of FASCAM (artillery scatterable mines). For every 5 yards crossed, a waster has a 5 in 20 chance of stepping on a mine (damage 3d20 to one leg if walking, Burst Radius 3, TN 5 to detect on *minesweeping* Aptitude). The only good news is that these mines are old and rusty and have a Reliability of 13.

A casual search shows most of the vehicles to be stripped, but a Hard (9) *scroungin'* roll turns up an SA SAW (reliability 15) with 20 rounds some 15 yards into the minefield. An Incredible (11) *scroungin'* roll finds an AT-80 (an SA version of the North's M-95 LGAT) deep (30 yards) in the battlefield.

The lucky finder of the AT-80 disturbs a cloud of rust mites that has been happily eating their way through the battlefield debris. Angered at being disturbed, they "attack" the scav who disturbed them.

Any loud shouting, like posse members being attacked by rust mites, may also awaken a 'glom that has formed from the bodies of LatAm soldiers who were unceremoniously dumped into a mass grave.

Rust Mites

Corporeal: D:2d6, N:2d10, Q:3d8, S:1d4, V:1d8

Fightin': brawlin' 3d10

Mental: C:1d4, K:1d4, M:1d4, Sm:1d4, Sp:1d4

Search 3d10, overawe 4d6

Pace: 12

Size: 10 (10' diameter cloud)

Wind: NA

Terror: 3

Special Abilities:

   Flight: Pace 12

   Metallophagic: After a successful attack against a metal object, each action following exposure reduces Durability by 1d6.

   Weakness–Magnets: Magnets disorient and repel mites. Small magnets repel for 6". Larger ones up to 2 feet.

   Only harmed by area effect weapons: Each wound inflicted reduces the diameter of the dust-mite cloud by one foot.

Description: These bugs appear as a red haze that move towards the posse, devouring any metal carried by the scavengers.

'Glom

Corporeal: D:2d6, N:2d6, Q:3d8, S:2d12+6, V:2d12+6

Fightin': brawlin' 6d6, shootin': pistol, rifle, smg 3d6

Mental: C:2d10, K:1d6, M:1d12+4, Sm:1d6, Sp:1d8

Overawe: 5d12+4

Pace: 6

Size: 18

Wind: 26

Terror: 11

Special Abilities:

   Damage Resistance: Any time the 'glom is wounded, not only must the location of the hit be resolved, but the exact body that's hit must be determined as well. For example, one shot might land in the gizzards of the first body, and another in the gizzards of a different body. These wounds are *not* cumulative! To use a shortcut method to track this, you can give the 'glom hits for each component body. Component bodies take damage as if they were Size 6; use Size 12 for massive attacks.

   Undead: Focus—core brain. One of the bodies is the original core of the 'glom. If the heroes can somehow figure out which head holds the core brain and destroy it, they can drop the abomination without resorting to weapons of mass destruction. In order to use any mind-affecting power, a syker must know which is the core brain and target it specifically. Trial and error is an acceptable method of finding the core brain, by the way.

   Weapons: The glom is well armed, wielding two NA Commando SMGs (15 rounds each), one pump shotgun (3 rounds), and a NA officer's sidearm (5 rounds). It can fire each weapon on every action. In addition, it's three other bodies are armed with crowbars, broken entrenching tools, and other instruments of head-bashing (STR+1d6).

Description: This horror looks like a conglomeration of bodies melded into a single mass of putrid flesh. Arms, legs, and heads stick out at all different angles around the abomination, and the heads mutter and gibber constantly producing a mixed cacophony of voices.

This Just Keeps Getting Better...

As the posse moves south they begin to encounter bands of 1d20 walkin' dead shambling south. They attack any living creatures dumb enough to mess with them. Use the standard walkin' dead stats from the *Hell on Earth* rulebook for these speed bumps. How many of these bands they run into is up to you, Marshal, but we recommend at least a couple; don't use too many, though, or the players are liable to get bored with zombie stomping!

More importantly, tell any Harrowed in the posse that he feels a strange sensation on a Hard (9) *Cognition* roll. It seems to be a gentle tug to the south.

Any Harrowed sleeping in Globe suffers from *night terrors* as the manitou array at B2 pulls at him (if they already have *night terrors* their *Vigor* roll is at *-2*). Describe the dream as being in the ocean as an undertow pulls them out to sea to a gleaming white temple.

As they draw nearer to GAIA, any Harrowed in the posse feels almost as if he is a fish slowly being reeled in on a line. The deader's manitou seems to whisper louder, and the flutter in his chest struggles harder than normal to escape its cage of bone. However, Marshal, be careful to say the sensations intensify as the hero heads *south* and not towards GAIA; you don't want to tip your hand too soon!

Zombie Oracle

Oracle, AZ: Fear Level 3

Oracle, AZ is only a place name on a map after GAIA got done with it in the late 2040's. The "town" consists of a crossroads with an old battered sign on the northward road reading:

Gersholm Agricultural Industrial
Advancement
Oracle, Arizona Facility
No Trespassing—Violators will be
Prosecuted

A Fair (5) *trackin'* roll reveals recent vehicular traffic has gone up the north road (the Globe traders), along with more shod and bare human feet than the tracker can count. An Onerous (7) result on the same roll reveals that some of the feet were missing toes or were otherwise dragged—as if the owners were lame (these are the tracks of zombies).

Harrowed who reach this point must make a Dominion check at +2 for the manitou and adjust their Dominion points appropriately as if this was a beginning of session. From this point on, as long as the Harrowed is within 5 miles of B2, any Fate Chips spent by the Marshal for Dominion should count as one color higher, with blue chips giving the manitou control for 2 hours. The manitou's Dominion checks continue to be at +2 for any attempts it makes to control its host.

Now, That's a Lotta Zombies!

Biosphere2, AZ: Fear Level 5

The posse heads up the road toward GAIA for 5 miles along a fairly well maintained stretch of highway. Nestled in the foothills of the Santa Catalina Mountains, untouched by the Last War, the spectacular view may take the posse's breath away—if the horde of zombies surrounding the security fence doesn't take it first.

As the posse tops a rise, the B2 campus is spread out below them. This is a good time to give the heroes a map of the site. The Biosphere itself sits in the center, surrounded by support and outbuildings, the whole of which is surrounded by an electrified 10' tall security fence. Around this is the biggest horde of walkin' dead the posse has ever seen—unless they have been across the Mississippi to Necropolis! (But then, no one has been there and returned, so that's impossible.)

Several hundred walkin' dead, from zombie receptionist to reanimated tank drivers, ring the fence, and their combined moans and screams of frustration can be heard from the posse's vantage point. Don't forget the Fear Level 5 here, Marshal!

The scene is awe inspiring—Incredible (11) TN *guts* checks are appropriate even if the posse has dealt with walkin' dead before and are jaded toward the living-impaired.

The groaning mass presses toward the fence, and though most are smart enough not to electrocute themselves, some eventually give in to the station's siren-like emissions and attempt to jump the barrier. The smell of scorched flesh fills the air as these zombies twist and jerk from the high voltage. More just keep shambling in from the surrounding desert.

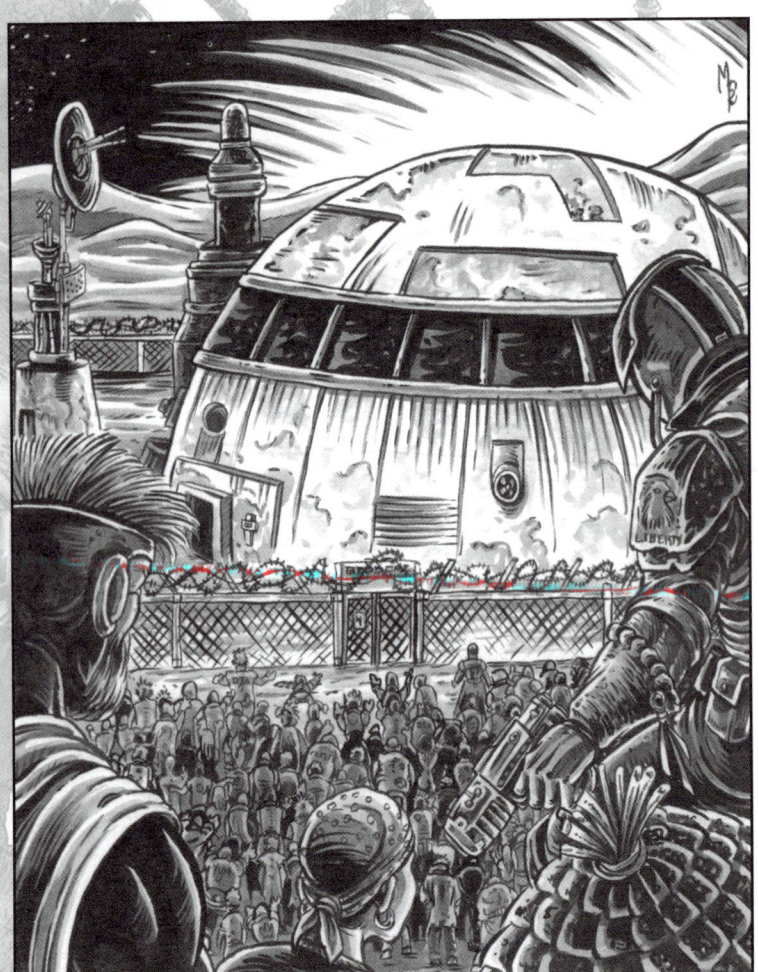

not waste time trying to score headshots, but are simply trying to slow the converging horde down long enough for the heroes to clear the gate.

Unless the heroes have access to flight, teleportation, or other method to bypass the intervening zombies, they have to fight their way in—the zombies encircle the entire compound. They should make it, but the difficulty is up to you, Marshal. At the very least, the heroes should face five or more zombies for every member of the group before they can clear the mass, even with the assistance from inside the compound.

Another option is to run this as a "narrative" combat. Describe the fight quickly but make it costly in terms of ammo and strain. Even barreling through with vehicles can be a problem—there are enough deaders here to gum up the wheels of tracked vehicles, let alone civilian cars.

Make the posse sweat, Marshal, but get 'em inside eventually.

We'll Take Our Chances Here, Thanks...

Should the posse decide that discretion is the better part of living and not attempt to enter the compound, you may have to provide a little "push," Marshal. Perhaps in the time they've been observing the mass, a pack of walkin' dead has cut them off from escape. Or maybe a 'glom or two, drawn by the MCA is moving up behind them.

A firefight outside the fence with either of those opponents momentarily overwhelms the lure of the MCA for a number of the deaders below. There's nothing like fresh brains, after all! Soon, the posse finds itself with only one safe haven in a storm of reanimated eating machines—the Biosphere 2.

The posse can see at least a couple dozen uniformed security guards patrolling the fence's inner perimeter watching for breaches. The guards appear to be well armed, but are not firing on the masses of undead just yards away.

You've Got To Be Kidding!

The guards notice the posse after a few minutes (especially if they arrive in vehicles), and begin waving to them. Obviously, the living folks inside the complex are trying to get the heroes to make a run for the complex.

If the posse attempts to enter the complex the guards begin shooting at the zombies outside the gate to clear a path. The guards are savvy enough to

GAIA Security Guards (30)

These troops are mostly the original staff from before Judgment Day, persuaded to stay here through the promise of security, stability, and a constant source of food. The guards wear black uniforms with the logo of GAIA on the shoulder, and seem well-armed with HI weapons. They are all loyal to Gersholm, although the press of zombies has many of them on the edge of sanity.

Profile: GAIA Security Guard

Corporeal: D:3d8 N:2d8 Q:2d10 S:1d8 V:2d6
Dodge 2d8, fightin': brawlin' 2d8, shootin': pistol, rifle, shotgun 3d8, sneak 2d8.
Mental: C:2d6 K:1d6 M:2d6 Sm:1d6 Sp:2d8
Guts 2d8, overawe 3d6
Wind: 14
Pace: 10
Edges: None
Hindrances: Obligation: GAIA
Gear: HI Thunderer, HI Blazer or HI Damnation or HI Devastator (12gauage caseless autoshotgun), 2 full clips each, walkie-talkie.

Bounty

Accepting Bradford's request: 1 white chip apiece.
Saving the traders: 1 white chip apiece.
Making it into the B2 Compound: 1 red chip apiece.

Chapter Two: Out of the Frying Pan ...

Once the posse makes it inside the B2 compound, they are met by a man who introduces himself as Corey Hartsoe, head of security at the GAIA project. He thanks the posse for coming, and asks if they are a relief force from Globe alerted by the recent trade convoy.

If questioned about all the walkin' dead, Corey says they started showing up in numbers within the last week or so, about the time the Globe trade convoy left.

Sharp-eyed wasters might recognize the HI weapons the guards are using as similar to those employed by the Combine. Hartsoe explains the firearms predate the Last War and reassures the heroes that neither he nor anyone else in the compound is associated with Throckmorton.

After the heroes have had ample time to talk to Hartsoe, he receives a call on his walkie-talkie from Gersholm, and asks the posse to follow him.

Dr. Gersholm, I Presume?

Hartsoe takes the heroes to the entrance of B2 where Dr. Gersholm is waiting for them. He thanks the posse for coming and seems unperturbed by the horde of zombies surrounding his "Barony." He offers his hospitality, taking the crew to the Human Habitat module of B2 and providing them an opportunity to get cleaned up and change clothes if they desire. He then invites the posse for a tour of the Biosphere and then dinner.

Baron Gersholm is accompanied at all times by two bodyguards. Use the profile for the GAIA security guards found in the last chapter.

Dr. Hans Aubrecht Gersholm—or the Baron as he prefers to be called now—is the driving force behind the GAIA project. Originally a disciple of the infamous Darious Hellstromme, Gersholm was a key part of the long-term HI project to harness the power of fear that has flooded the globe for the last 200 years, although even now he doesn't reveal this fact.

Gersholm's area of expertise is in the field of spirit fetters used to power cyborgs and the like. He is also an expert in botany, and before the Last War had studied several of the plant-like creatures created by the Reckoners.

Finding himself with a well-stocked agricultural facility after the Big Bang, Gersholm has become a power to be reckoned with. He uses his foodstuffs to secure high-tech salvage items from nearby communities so his experiments to continue.

Profile: Dr. Hans Gersholm

Corporeal: D:2d6 N:3d6 Q:2d8 S:4d4 V:2d10

Dodge 3d10, shootin': pistol 3d6

Mental: C:4d8 K:2d12 M:2d6 Sm:3d12 Sp:2d10

Academia: occult 4d12, guts 2d10, search 2d8, science: occult engineering 5d12, science: botany 3d12, science: biology 3d12, scrutinize 5d8,

Wind: 20

Pace: 6

Size: 6

Edges: Arcane background: junker 3 (ex-mad scientist)

Hindrances: Bad eyes 3, geezer 5 (87 years old), loco 4

Gear: Experimental HI plasma pistol (as the junker weapon but with a Stability 20)

Description: Dr. Gersholm appears as a fragile, older man with thinning white hair and thick glasses perched on his nose. His speech has a slight German accent. He's always dressed in a voluminous, spotless, white lab coat—which nicely conceals his plasma pistol.

How Does Your Garden Grow?

Left to his devices, Doctor—now Baron—Gersholm likely will edge slowly down the road toward being a servitor of Famine. How does this happen to a man who is providing food to half the survivor communities in Arizona and New Mexico?

Prior to the Last War, Gersholm was involved in spirit fetter research and saw the potential for a variety of applications for powering things other than cyborgs. Gersholm had perfected the building of spirit fetters as a method of promoting plant growth. Plants cultivated in this fashion reach incredible size in an unbelievably short period of time. The yield per plant is also prodigious.

Unfortunately, the procedure exposes the plants to energy from the Hunting Grounds that makes the plants carriers of the faminite disease. The amount per plant is small, so the effect is insidious, slowly building up in the victim's system. The more tainted veggies a person eats the quicker they become a faminite. Gersholm is as yet unaware of the side effect, but that doesn't make him an innocent in the affair.

Gersholm continues to create Tethered Organic Fertilization Units to help his garden grow. Since the TOFUs use spirit fetters to harness the manitous, they also require a host cadaver as well. Now, folks aren't considerate enough to die at convenient times for the good doctor, so he has to "hurry" the process along by killing any wanderer unfortunate enough to stumble onto GAIA. And, because reanimated victims might be a bit of a hassle, he pares the bodies down to the bare essentials—the head.

Biosphere2 Tour

Baron Gersholm escorts the posse to the second floor of the Human Habitat, offering suites for them to settle in and get cleaned up. He offers a tour and dinner in an hour, after the heroes are refreshed. A guard is left in the center stairwell to see to any needs of the posse.

As promised, the Baron returns in an hour and gives the posse a tour of the B2 complex. During the tour, the Baron gives them a little history of B2—minus the urban legends and horrible truth behind the complex, of course!

Here's a quick summary of what is in each section of B2.

Lung (1)

The lung of B2 provides a way for the air volume within the structure to expand and contract without causing the facility to explode from the changing air pressure. In addition, the ability to control the height of each lung allows the stimulation of airflow within the Biosphere.

Each lung consists of a huge domed structure with a tough, rubber-like membrane stretched across the bottom. Under the membrane is a tunnel that leads to the basement of the main B2 complex, allowing for air exchange between the two structures. Baron Gersholm does not take the posse to the lung, but describes its use to them if asked.

The lung may provide a way out of B2 when the horde of zombies makes it inside later. Come on, you knew it was coming!

Human Habitat (2)

The entrance to B2 is located in this section through an airlock-type door.

This three-story area houses the living area and workshop for the Baron and his closest henchmen. Attached to the top of the Human Habitat is a huge antennae array, which looks to be of post-war manufacture. Currently, the Baron and his two bodyguards are the only inhabitants.

First Floor. This level contains a dining hall, kitchen, living room, control room, and library containing hundreds of slugs of not only scientific data but

also movies, vid shows, books, and other entertainment relics of the world long-gone.

The control room has readouts for 750 sensors that monitor the vital statistics of this living laboratory. The sensors measure temperature, light, humidity, carbon dioxide and other qualities of the air and soil. In response to these readings, operators can, for example, turn on blowers for cooling and heating or create a miniature rainstorm to change the humidity. B2's own ghost-rock reactor provides heating and cooling and is controlled from here.

Second floor. There are several suites of rooms arranged around the central stairwell. The Baron offers rooms here to the heroes for their stay. Each suite has a bathroom with running hot water, towels, clean sheets, and all the amenities of pre-War 21st century life.

Third floor. This is the Baron's workshop. Huge humming machines fill the room, their low buzz making the posse's ears ache (Harrowed have a

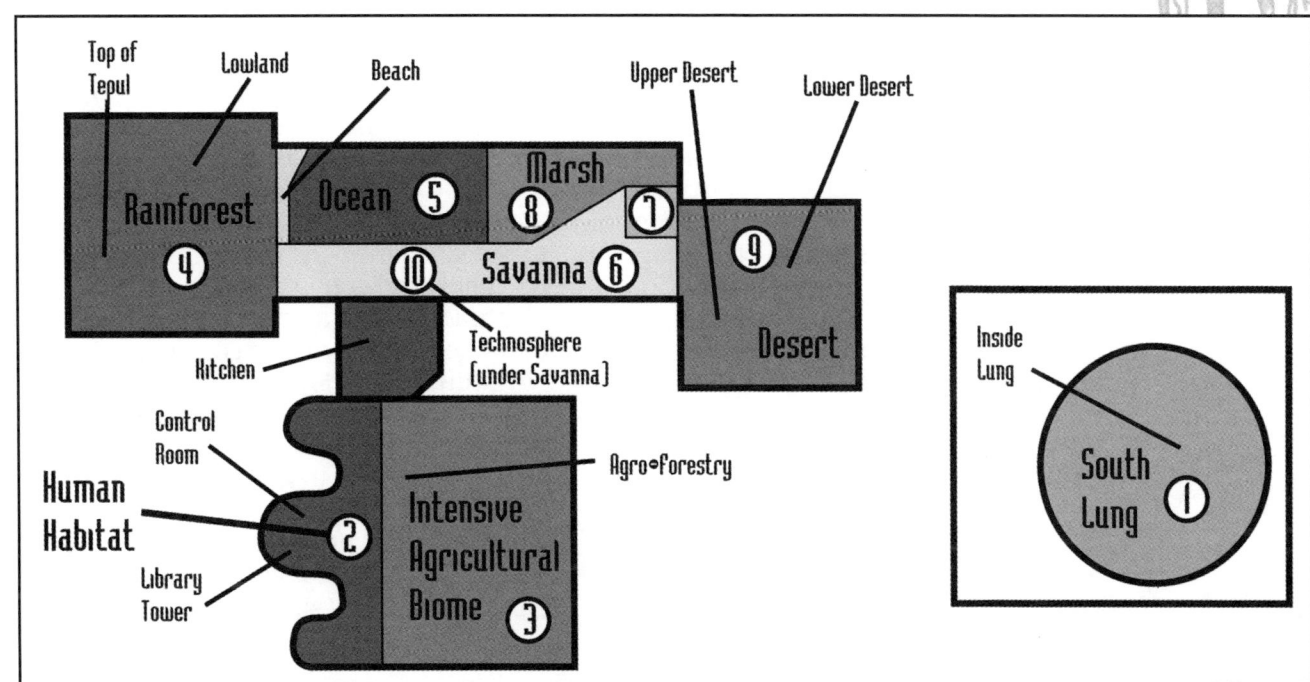

splitting headache in this room). These are the capacitors for the spirit array on the roof, which draws in manitous for later fettering in his Tethered Organic Fertilization Units.

A side effect of this intense spiritual field is that sykers' meridians are disrupted, causing all their powers to cost double normal Strain. The Glow and toxic favors are unaffected.

Scattered across the tables are a variety of devices in various stages of assembly. Anyone who makes an Hard (9) *science: occult engineering* realizes that these appear to be spirit fetters. If questioned about them, Gersholm says he met a cyborg a few months ago and was intrigued at the possibility of the devices. These are merely an academic exercise to pass the time.

The basement access door is locked, and only Gersholm knows the combination, although a persistent posse with an electronic lockpick could get the door open with a Hard (9) *lockpicking* roll. The Baron does not take them into this section.

Basement. This level is divided into three sections.

The first is the Baron's main workshop. This is the old infirmary, now converted to act as an assembly line for the Baron's Tethered Organic Fertilization Units. The walls are covered in cabinets, and several gurneys (a number equal to the posse) fill the room. A wide variety of surgical instruments are present, along with a number of completed spirit fetters. Also along the walls are a number of cabinets that hum with the sound of high voltage. Any stray shots have a 1 in 6 chance of hitting these capacitors, causing an arc of electricity to shoot out 3 yards for 3d8 points of damage.

An old storage/maintenance room has been divided in half with chain link fencing. Inside the chain-link enclosure are 7 walkin' dead the Baron has collected for study (see the end of this adventure for the profile).

Outside the enclosure, chained to the wall, is a single walkin' dead that the Baron has had limited success in "taming." It is the body of Gersholm's original Security Chief and one of the Baron's only friends. He calls the abomination by its original name (Bud), and has even taught it to speak again, although it is rudimentary at best. Anyone getting a look at Bud's restraints notices that Gersholm is dangerously negligent in his precautions; all it takes is a Hard (9) *Strength* roll to break them!

A corridor leads to the Rainforest biome. Next to this door is a diagram of the basement level. Heroes who make a Fair (5) *Cognition* roll notice the route from here to the Rainforest and the tunnel from the Savannah to the Lungs.

The last room on this level is the old cold storage room, originally used for storage of the crew's perishable foodstuffs. Now it is used to store not only food but also the bodies of those whose heads have been used to make Tethered Organic Fertilization Units. There are currently three bodies awaiting grinding into plant food, along with three tubs of hamburger awaiting delivery to the biome fields.

IAB (3)

The Intensive Agricultural Biome provides much of the food planned to be sent to Globe and beyond by the Baron. Here his greatest technological triumph's success can be seen. The fields are covered with a variety of crops, all of tremendous size. The noise of muffled, unidentifiable sounds may be heard here on a Fair (5) *Cognition* roll. The sounds are made by the TOFU heads attempting to scream; since the severed heads have no lungs and tongues make lousy diaphragms, glottal smacks and clicks are about all they can accomplish.

Another Fair (5) *Cognition* roll spots several 1' diameter plastic or styrofoam domes planted in the ground throughout the area. The Baron Gersholm explains that these are speakers that provide music and noise to the plants, helping them grow to such prodigious size. Several workers move through the fields tending the crops.

Gersholm doesn't let the posse inspect the "speakers." He waxes poetic about his advances in the fields of plant growth and TOFU use, but quickly bores most wasters. Should the posse ask what "TOFU" means, he explains it's a highly technical acronym that would be meaningless to anyone but another botanist of his background.

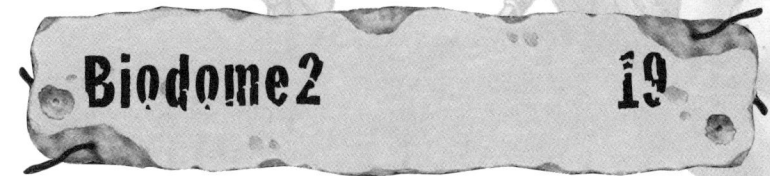
Rainforest (4)

The tropical rainforest biome of B2 is 2000 sq. meters in area, and 28 meters high at its highest point. A simulated equatorial climate supports plant species from the humid tropical regions of the world.

This was designed to simulate a highland cloud forest. Lowland rainforest includes most of the eastern part of the biome. Large trees with a ground layer of ferns and other tropical low-lying plants dominate the area. This biome is very hot and humid, and mist makes it hard to see further than 5 feet. Banana trees, plantains, and coffee trees can be glimpsed through breaks in the mist.

Gersholm does not allow the posse to stray from the path in this biome during the tour. The heroes may notice there are no "speakers" hidden among the foliage here. This requires an Onerous (7) *Cognition* roll unless a player specifically asks.

Ocean (5)

The Biosphere2 ocean is a 900,000 gallon Caribbean reef-model ecosystem complete with a wide variety of aquatic creatures, from microscopic organisms to top-level predators, including several small sharks. Should the posse decide to go for a swim, they might run into these eating machines if they venture into the deeper water.

Savannah (6)

This biome contains a variety of terrain and plant life, including a savanna stream with mostly gum trees and wet-land plants, a granite orchard, fruit trees, and, of course, tall grasses, which Baron Gersholm explains are experimental wheat hybrids he hopes

will be able to grow in the wasteland and alleviate the famine facing the survivors of the Last War.

The heroes may hear muffled sounds here similar to those in the IAB on an Onerous (7) *Cognition* roll. If questioned, Gersholm says he has the speaker system installed throughout the Savannah to help the wheat grow. Gersholm also points to several sacks of seed wheat that he proudly points to as the future of agriculture in Arizona. These are a new plant (*pentatriticale*) that is basically a five-lobed hybrid of wheat and rye, possessing a rapid growth and high yield.

Actually, Gersholm has seeded this area with more of the TOFUs. They are deep in the grasses, so Gersholm does not allow the posse to leave the path.

Thornscrub (7)

This biome has a variety of cacti and other succulents, forming a thorny barrier with tough grasses along the ground. The area next to the marsh is covered in a variety of vegetables, including some huge tomato and bean plants. Once again, muffled noises can be heard from the foliage near some 1' diameter domes planted in the ground. As before, Baron Gersholm explains that these are speakers that provide music and noise to the plants, helping them grow to such prodigious size.

Besides the TOFUs, there is nothing of interest to the posse in this biome. Anyone trying to push through the spiky and prickly plants that line the area must make an Incredible (11) *Nimbleness* roll or take Wind equal to the amount she misses the TN from the thorns.

The upper area, next to the Savannah, provides access to the Scrubber below. The hatch can be seen from the pathway with a Hard (9) *Cognition* roll.

Marsh (8)

Those wasters who come from Louisiana should feel right at home in this section. The cypress trees and enshrouding Spanish moss make this an eerie area even on the brightest day. The marsh provides the B2 inhabitants with a fishery stocked with catfish and other freshwater species.

Desert (9)

The desert resembles much of the Southwest, with a hot climate and little plant life. Several lizards can be seen basking in the sun, along with several species of desert cacti.

The World Below (10)

Beneath Biosphere2 are acres of pipe, wires, air handlers, and control systems, crisscrossing the entire complex in a maze that would confuse a minotaur. Most of these passages seem to be built for light-sensitive dwarves, being poorly lit (one 40 watt bulb every 30') and 4' high x 4' wide.

A tunnel leads from the basement lab storage/maintenance room of the Human Habitat to the Rainforest—exiting near the blood rose creepers, of course. An access way is also present in the Lower Savannah, through the Scrubber.

The Scrubber consists of a series of fans that blow air back and forth between the Lung and B2 in a tunnel that is large enough for a person to duck-walk through. Several electrostatic filters block the way, but these are easily removed with an Onerous (7) *Strength* check or a sharp knife. This is the only way for a man-sized creature to get to the lung underground from B2. Rumors and fears among the staff of *something* living in the basement have brought a small (Size 8) Lurker to life. Use the statistics from the *Hell on Earth* rulebook, but with *Strength* 4d12, Armor 3, and no Coup.

The Outside

The B2 complex is surrounded by several buildings, including a two-story guard barracks, a motor pool with two jeeps (each with one tank full of fuel), the ghost-rock reactor building, and several storage buildings filled with foodstuffs, spare parts, and assorted junk. The armory is located in the guard barracks and contains very little. Thirty rounds can be found for each weapon type (9mm caseless, 10mm caseless, and 12 gauge caseless), several spare batteries for the walkie-talkies, and 3 tasers.

Dinner Is Served

When they return to the Human Habitat, a fabulous meal has been prepared, consisting of fresh fish, vegetables of all types, and fruit pies for desert. The posse is also introduced to Greg Powell, a drifter who made his way to B2 a couple of days ago. Powell is a non-descript waster who stumbled in from the east ahead of the larger hordes of walkin' dead.

Unfortunately for the posse, all the food has been heavily laced with a slow-acting sedative drug. The posse feels full and sleepy as the night wears on, but not unduly so. Once asleep, however, they have a hard time waking up. Any posse member who ate the food attempting to stay awake must make an Incredible (11) *Vigor* or doze off as well.

Truly suspicious posses may have one or two members pass on the food Gersholm offers. If so, that's fine; they're just showing a healthy bit of paranoia in the post-Apocalyptic world!

Unjust Desserts

Around 2 AM, a squad of five guards burst into the heroes' rooms. Use the profiles from Chapter One for these goons.

Anyone asleep at this time must roll *Cognition* against an Incredible (11) TN or be surprised. *Light sleeper* and *heavy sleeper* modify that roll normally.

Posse members who partook of Gersholm's sedative-laced repast have a tougher time of it. Even once they make the *Cognition* roll (assuming they were asleep), they must then roll *Vigor* against an Incredible (11) TN to shake off the effects of the drug. Those who fail are at –2 to all rolls during the fight.

The guards use tasers on anyone who is awake. Once the target is stunned, the guards inject the hero with an anesthetic that renders him unconscious for the duration barring use of a power like *purge*.

Should the heroes be canny enough to defeat this ambush, they've got a chance to explore B2 more thoroughly—and without adult supervision! They don't have all night, though, because Gersholm is expecting the sedated heroes to arrive in his laboratory shortly. After a 20-minute wait, he puts the complex on alert and the remaining 15 guards who aren't on perimeter duty begin combing the complex for the heroes in groups of five. This time, they're shooting to kill.

To complicate the heroes' endeavors, Hartsoe closes and locks off interior doors from the control room in response to reports from his patrols in an attempt to channel the posse toward

the laboratory. Exactly which doors he shuts depends on the posse's route of escape, but use them and the guard patrols to force the heroes toward the final showdown in **Chapter Three**.

Bounty

Noting the odd noises from the TOFU units: 1 white chip to each hero who does.

Defeating the guards sent to capture them: 1 red chip to each hero who participates.

Chapter Three: This Isn't Fun Anymore

Coming into this chapter you're likely in one of two situations, Marshal: either the posse has succumbed to Gersholm's treachery, or they're running through B2 playing the monkey-in-the-wrench. We'll address the latter situation first, as we hope the posse was tough or smart enough not to fall for a little bit of drugged zucchini.

Flies in the Ointment

If the posse manages to short-circuit Gerhshom's plan, you've got a little maneuvering to do, Marshal. You might be lucky enough to have a nosy posse that runs right for the basement to find out what's really going on. On the other hand, your wasters may decide to head for the hills.

Should the heroes decide the second option is their best bet, remind them of the horde of undead just outside the fences. If that approach fails, you can use a more heavy-handed method to push the heroes toward Gersholm's lab with the guard patrols and electronically locking doors.

On the off-chance even that isn't enough, Hartsoe dumps pesticides into the ventilation system and routes it into the posse's location via the control room. Without a method to cancel the poisons, such as powers like *purge* or *immunity* (Smog) or even gas masks, each hero must make an Onerous (7) *Vigor* roll each round. Everyone that fails suffers 1d6 Wind, plus 1 Wind for each point they missed the TN; even if a waster succeeds, she suffers 1d6 Wind each round she's in the foul stuff.

That should be incentive enough to hustle them along!

Come into My Parlor...

No matter what time they arrive after the failed ambush, the posse finds the door to the basement area not only unlocked, but open! In the workshop, they find the Baron, his two bodyguards, and Greg Powell. The guards are aiming their weapons at the posse when they enter, thanks to warning from Hartsoe. Moments behind the posse arrive the remaining guard patrols to cut off escape.

The Baron calls to the posse to surrender, as the situation is hopeless. If a fight breaks out at this point, Marshal, assume his bodyguards have a card up their sleeves in the first round, but the rest of the guards don't. Head on to the **Firefight!** section.

At this point, the Baron is only too happy to demonstrate the care and use of the Tethered Organic Fertilization Units, and informs the posse that it will be a great asset to the cornfield in the IAB. He implants the first Tethered Organic Fertilization Unit into Greg Powell, killing him with a lethal injection then quickly opening the back of his head and implanting a spirit

fetter. The doctor then hooks Powell up to the manitou capacitor array, capturing a manitou instantly. What was once Greg Powell opens his eyes.

Gersholm then cuts off Powell's head and places it into a steel bucket. While this is happening the guards, having never seen this done, are riveted to the spectacle and only notice anything the posse does on a Hard (9) *Cognition* roll.

Unless your wasters have a thing for being made into decapitated-head fertilizer, odds are they're going to put up a fight at this point. If they do, Marshal, head on to **Firefight!**; otherwise, Gersholm has his guards disarm the heroes and strap them to gurneys—landing them in the same place they'd have been had they not resisted the first ambush! See **Snooze and Lose**, below.

Snooze and Lose

If all goes according to the Baron's plan, the heroes awake some time later in his basement lab, secured to gurneys with IVs in their arms. Gersholm demonstrates his plans for the posse on Powell, as in **Come into My Parlor**.

Presumably, the posse won't sit around passively and wait their turn at becoming plant lamps. An Incredible (11) *Strength* roll is required to break the bonds on the gurneys, an Incredible (11) *Nimbleness* lets the hero slip her restraints, while a similar *Deftness* roll allows the waster to work the release on the straps. No doubt the heroes may have a number of useful arcane abilities here as well. However, remember that sykers have their Strain costs doubled due to interference from the manitou capacitor array, while the Glow and toxic favors function normally.

The posse's gear is simply piled in the corner, should they get free. Head on to the next section for the basement battle.

Firefight!

The guards use their tasers first, as Gersholm needs the heroes alive to conduct the TOFU implantation. However, none of the GAIA inhabitants has a death wish, so the guards are also armed with HI Thunderers and Blazers, which they readily use should things get nasty.

Don't forget every stray round has a chance of hitting a dangerous piece of electrical equipment, Marshal; the Baron hasn't! Throughout the firefight, Gersholm shouts "Stop! Stop! You'll damage the machinery!"

All this commotion upsets Bud in the next room and he jerks himself free from the restraints. He quickly frees the other walkin' dead and moves toward the sounds of fighting.

If no shot hits the equipment before then, in the third round of combat, a stray bullet or taser wire from a guard's weapon smacks into one of the capacitators, causing it to short out. As soon as one of the capacitators shorts, the feedback blows the power mains for the entire complex—and that spells trouble for everybody, since the electric fences are no longer protecting the compound!

About that time, Bud and the other walkin' dead shamble into the darkened room and begin attacking everyone in smell.

Lights Out

After the gunfire dies down, screams can be heard from the bodyguards' radios over the crackle of fire in the electronics closet. It sounds like the zombies are swarming the fence and entering the compound now that the electricity to the fence is off.

The sounds of dying guards being torn apart continue for several minutes until the last are eaten by the zombie horde. In the ensuing slaughter, one of the perimeter guards tries to enter by hitting the airlock override, opening both doors and allowing the zombies entrance to the Biosphere.

The posse is now at Zombie Ground Zero.

Stand and Fight

If the heroes are shoot-out minded, they've got their hands more than full. There are over 400 walkin' dead and veteran walkin' dead pouring toward and into the complex, not to mention a

'glom or two. Trying to stand this horde down is going to get them dead fast! On the other hand, it does give them an opportunity to kill walkin' dead in everyone of Earth's environments save the artic in a single day.

It's up to you how hard you want to hit the heroes, Marshal. We recommend going easy at first and quickly escalating; maybe a zombie per hero at first, and then slowly doubling that number over a couple of rounds. That way, they have a chance to figure out how deep the corpse water is before they drown in it!

Bug Out!

There are too many possible options for escape from B2 to list here, but we've provided a couple of guidelines. Whatever route the heroes take, Marshal, make sure they understand just how bad the situation is. This should be a very tense run for their lives!

A straight charge for the outside through the doors is the toughest. Before they can break out, the heroes are probably going to face somewhere in the neighborhood of 100 zombies. Given the proximity of B2 to Phoenix, no small number of these are armed with military firearms (but not much ammunition!).

Blasting through the B2 dome is an option. The dome is pretty tough, having been reinforced by Hellstromme Industries, when it took over the project. The dome wall is AV 5, and takes 60 points of damage to blow a 2'x2' hole into the plexi-glass. As if that isn't work enough, the posse still has to hold off about 20 zombies inside while plugging away at the dome, and another 30 outside once they get free.

Posses who go underground into the basement have the best chance by going out through the lung, since it's removed enough to avoid the bulk of zombies. Maybe two or three zombies per hero attack the posse total throughout the course of the escape, and these come in small groups or individually.

Any delays result in more and more zombies converging on the heroes.

If the heroes haven't uncovered the secret of GAIA yet, you may want to have a waster fleeing through areas with TOFUs kick one over, revealing the shrieking head within, planted in the ground (Onerous (7) *Guts* check).

On the Road Again

As the sun comes up, the GAIA facility is overrun with a sea of walkin' dead. Hopefully, the posse is clear of the area. The compound is lost to the dead without a major expenditure of ammunition, and even then, the reactor soon suffers a meltdown due to the system overload and lack of preventative measures (everyone who knew how is now zombie food!).

The journey back to Globe involves evading hordes of brain-hungry walkin' dead. The swarms are active in a 5-mile radius around B2. Once clear of this area, however, the trip should be uneventful, although walkin' dead are drawn to Oracle for the next few days, and an evil Marshal may have the posse encounter a few bands on the trip north.

Back at Globe

Globe is devastated by the news of the demise of GAIA, although if the posse has brought a sack of the new wonder wheat from the Savannah they might be able to salvage their town.

If they didn't bring back any seed—and who can really blame them with a zombie riot going on—Rebecca may ask the heroes to help the town find another way to alleviate the famine.

If the heroes decide to dig in the battlefields themselves, use the **Phoenix Salvage Table** (created by *HOE* Master John Hopler) at the end of this adventure.

Tellin' Tales

The posse must be careful with their story of what happened at the facility to avoid a panic with stories of a zombie army on the march! Earning a Legend Chip for their tale of the defeat of the zombie horde at Oracle requires a careful spin by the posse's tale-tellers. Any attempts at *tale-tellin'* are a level higher than normal, thanks to the care with which the teller has to weave his story of victory over the forces of the supernatural.

Bounty

Posse discovers the secret of the TOFUs: 1 white chip
Posse defeats Gersholm: 1 red chip
Posse escapes B2: 1 blue chip
Posse takes a bag(s) of seed wheat from Savannah: 1 blue chip

Phoenix Salvage Table

Roll 1d10. Add +2 to the total for each raise on your hero's *scroungin'* roll. The battlefield has been picked over fairly well, so the base TN for the *scroungin'* roll is Hard (9).

Roll	Salvage
1	**Fatigues:** A set of slightly moldy, but serviceable fatigues. (Roll 1d6: 1-3 Mexican, 4-6 CSA)
2	**Backpack:** A military issue backpack with quick-release straps.
3	**Combat knife:** Treat as a large knife. There is a compass in the pommel and the handle holds 1d20 strike-anywhere matches, 50' of fishing line, and 2 fish hooks.
4	**Fusil-20:** The standard issue Mexican rifle. (Ammo 5.45mm, Shots 30, Speed 1, ROF 9, Range 20, Damage 5d6).
5	**SA Assault Rifle**
6	**Helmet:** A standard infantry helmet.
7	**First aid kit:** The kit has gauze, bandages, antiseptic, 1d6 shots of pain killer, and 1 course of antibiotics.
8	**Ammo Can:** The can contains 0 to 90 rounds (1d10-1 x 10). Roll 1d6 for type: 1: 7.62mm, 2: 5.45mm, 3: .50 pistol, 4: 9mm, 5: 50 machine-gun, 6: .45 ACP.
9	**Military Radio:** Roll 1d6 for type: 1: Headset, 2-3: Walkie-talkie, 4: Backpack Unit, 5:Vehicular radio, 6: Military Base Set.
10	**SA M-50**
11	**Infantry Battlesuit**
12	**Grenades:** 1d4 grenades. Roll 1d6 for type: 1: Frag, 2: Smoke, 3: 40mm frag, 4: 40mm HEDP, 5: 40mm Inferno, 5: 40mm Flechette, 6: 40mm Smoke.
13	**Laser Designator:** A working laser designator (Speed 1, Range 50).
14	**Mk 40:** CSA automatic grenade launcher (Ammo 40mm, Shots 30, Speed 1, ROF 3, Range 20, Damage by grenade type).
15	**M-82 RAW HEAT:** CSA single-shot, disposable, antitank rocket. (Ammo 140mm rocket, Shots 1, Speed 2, ROF 1, Range 40, Damage 4d20 AP 4).
16	**M-510 Hornet:** CSA disposable surface-to-air missile. (Ammo 154mm missile, Shots 1, Speed 2, ROF 1, Range 70", Damage 4d12 Burst 10, Sensor 3d8).

The Armory: Guns o' the South

Everybody's heard of Winchester, Colt, and Remington, but all of those companies are Yankee gun makers. Sure, a goodly number of firearms produced north of the Mason-Dixon creep into the South by way of the Disputed Territories, the Maze, or even St. Louis. However, if the only guns the Confederacy could get its hands on were Union-made, the War would have ended a long time ago!

Second Place

The truth is, the Confederacy had a tough go of it at first. In a two-country arms race, they were a distant second. At the beginning of the War, around 60 private companies in the Union produced firearms; in the South, there were none of any size. Major Josiah Gorgas, the head of the Confederate Bureau of Ordinance, had a big job ahead of him!

Luckily for the Confederacy, Gorgas got a couple of early breaks. However, while Fate seemed to favor his endeavors, Gorgas himself deserves much credit for the South's nearly miraculous arms mobilization. The man proved a master in juggling resources and motivating incredible results.

Government Armories

Major (long since made General) Gorgas' first break came in the form of machinery seized from the Maryland Harper's Ferry armory. He set up factories in Fayetteville and Asheville North Carolina and Richmond, Virginia, to use the Harper's Ferry equipment and dies. As the War progressed, Gorgas also set up major production facilities in Alabama and Texas.

Unfortunately, while Southern armorers proved quite proficient at copying Northern arms and manufacturing dies, this method left them always a step behind the Union.

Another drawback was the initial shortage of raw materials. Confederate supplies of steel were nearly nonexistent, requiring Gorgas' armorers to use iron or brass instead. Before long, the Confederates were reduced to cannibalizing candlesticks and church bells for brass!

Before this dire shortage could paralyze the Confederate war machine, the British and French broke the Union blockade and opened up the overseas markets to the South. First cotton and tobacco and later ghost rock purchased enough steel from Europe to keep Confederate armories rolling.

Some of the most famous foreign-made weapons are the unique LeMat pistols and carbines, the excellent Whitworth rifle, and the Martini-Henry rifle. These weapons helped keep the Confederate soldier armed in the middle years of the War.

Foreign Arms

At the same time Major Gorgas was struggling to get Confederate armories on their feet, Caleb Huse was purchasing arms abroad for the South. Although the Union was (and still is) the leading arms manufacturer in the world, several foreign firms provided top-quality firearms to the South.

Private Firms

As in any capitalistic society, eventually free enterprise took over. Where no private arms manufacturers of any size existed prior to the onset of the War, nearly 25 had sprung up in the South by 1865. Not all were successful, but many remain today.

Southern Shootin' Irons

Weapon	Shots	Caliber	ROF	Damage	Range Increment	Price
Carbines						
LeMat Carbine	9	.42	1	3d6	15	$35
& Shotgun	1	16-gauge	1	Special	5	—
Morse Carbine	1	.50	1	4d8	10	$18
"Richmond" Carbine	1	.52	1	4d8	15	$15
S & B Repeating Carbine	6	.44	2	3d8	10	$40
Pistols, Single-Action						
Gunnison Independence	6	.45	1	3d6	10	$14
L & R Navy	6	.36	1	2d6	10	$12
LeMat Grapeshot Pistol	9	.40	1	2d6	10	$25
& Shotgun	1	16-gauge	1	Special	5	—
LeMat Navy Pistol	9	.35	1	2d6	10	$25
& Shotgun	1	28-gauge	1	Special	5	—
Tyler Alamo	6	.44	1	3d6	10	$19
Pistols, Double-Action						
Adams & Deane Revolver	5	.44 C&B	2	3d6	10	$18
Gunnison Rubicon	6	.45	2	3d6	10	$14
Kerr Revolver Model 72	5	.44	2	3d6	10	$15
S & B Tornado	6	.36	2	2d6	10	$12
Rifles						
Cook Stars & Bars	1	.45	1	4d8	25	$21
Mk 1 Snider/Enfield	1	.58	1	5d8	25	$25
Martini-Henry Rifle	1	.45	1	4d8	25	$25
Tyler Texan	16	.44	1	4d8	20	$29
Whitworth	1	.45	1	4d8	30	$120
Shotguns						
Morse Lever-Action	5	12-gauge	1	Special	10	$40

Most of the early Confederate arms makers patterned their designs after successful Union firearms. Leech & Ridgon, Spiller & Burr, and Gunnison all got their start producing Colt Army or Navy revolver copies. Gunnison continues to follow the designs of the Northern arms manufacturer—so closely, in fact, that only an experienced gunsmith (or gunslinger) can tell the difference at a glance. Spiller & Burr has moved on to its own models, often with mixed results.

Cook & Brother, the most successful Southern gun maker primarily pursues government contracts, leaving the private citizen to his own devices for firearms. Cook rifles are among the most common weapons on the Confederate front lines, outside of the Martini-Henry imports.

A few of Gorgas original armories have privatized as well. Of these, the Tyler Ordnance Works has had the most luck. It's Texan rifle and Alamo pistol are popular among the Rangers, thanks to high capacity and similar cartridges—not to mention the names!

Individual Weapon Notes

Adams & Deane Revolver. This finely crafted, English-made, cap-and-ball pistol was once the weapon of choice for discerning Confederate officers. With the advent of cartridge pistols, it would have been soon relegated to museums if not for its spurless-hammer, which makes it much easier to fire from within a pocket. Many gunslingers keep the weapon as a holdout gun. Any attempts to conceal the A&D receive a +2 bonus to the *sneak* roll.

Cook Stars & Bars. After the Martini-Henry from which it's modeled, this is the most common weapon in Confederate service. In time, it may even replace the import rifle.

Gunnison Independence. This is little more than a single-action Colt Peacemaker with a different name.

Gunnison Rubicon. Like the Independence, the Rubicon is simply a Colt rip-off, this time in double-action.

Kerr Revolver. This English import is the standard sidearm issued to Confederate Army officers.

Leech & Rigdon Navy. A cartridge version of an earlier model (which was a Southern version of the Colt Navy), the L&R is fairly standard issue for the Confederate Navy sidearm.

LeMat Carbine. This is a larger, longer-barrel, stocked version of the LeMat pistol. Like it's smaller brother, the gun has a shotgun barrel under the carbine barrel. Only one or the other may be fired at a time.

LeMat Grapeshot Pistol. This is the same pistol described in the *Weird West Player's Guide*, page 78. It's popular among Confederate cavalrymen thanks to its high capacity and shotgun round, and a personal favorite of General J.E.B. Stuart. Originally a cap-and-ball weapon, its design has been refurbished to handle cartridges for many years now.

LeMat Navy Pistol. A lighter-weight, smaller-caliber version of the LeMat Grapeshot designed to fit the requirements of a CSA Navy request. Its smaller shotgun does less damage than its larger cousins. Modify normal shotgun damage as follows: Contact 5d6; 1-10 yards 4d6; 11-20 yards 3d6; 21-30 yards 2d6; 31+ yards 1d6.

Mk 1 Snider/Enfield. This is essentially an old 1853 Enfield Rifle Musket converted to metallic cartridges. No longer in front-line Confederate military service, it's still found in the hands of veterans and garrison troops. It uses a special ammunition ($5 for 50 rounds), and is incompatible with other ..58 caliber rounds. This rifle accepts a bayonet.

Martini-Henry. A single-shot, breechloading rifle, the Martini-Henry is the standard-issue rifle for both the British and Confederate armies. The British believe soldiers armed with repeaters would quickly waste ammunition, while the Confederates have yet to develop the industrial capacity to support high-magazine reapeaters like the Union. Cook &

Brother has begun producing ammunition for this weapon, which is imcompatible with most .45 rounds. The Martini-Henry (and its twin, the Stars & Bars) can mount a bayonet.

Morse Carbine. This is one of the earliest original Confederate designs. It's both cartridge-fed and breech-loading, making it a favorite cavalry weapon in the mid- to late 1860s. Further advances have pushed the Morse out of favor, but it can still be found in the hands of private citizens.

Morse Lever-Action Shotgun. Another innovative design from Morse Firearms, the Lever-Action Shotgun is designed for use in the Eastern trenches. It has a high magazine capacity and can mount a bayonet as well, making it well-suited for close-combat assaults. However, the lever occasionally locks, jamming the weapon. It has a Reliability of 19; a failure indicates a jam requiring a round and a Fair (5) *tinkerin'* or *trade: gunsmith* to fix.

Richmond Carbine. This weapon is an example of weaponry produced at Gorgas' early government armories. It is very similar in design to the Sharps carbine, but uses a smaller rounds. Like the Sharps, it was originally cap-and-ball, but over time, most have been converted to cartridge weapons. It's odd caliber shows a common problem with Confederate weapons: commonality of ammunition—as in there is very little. For all his talents, Gorgas had little luck standardizing a caliber for issue.

S & B Revolving Carbine. This fast-firing short rifle looks like a Colt pistol with big britches. It has a long barrel, stock, and foregrip, but uses a revolving cylinder to provide repeating fire. The odd design forces it to use special ammunition ($5 for a box of 50), that is somewhat less powerful than most full-size rounds. Its breech breaks open to allow quicker reloads. A cowpoke can reload 3 bullets in a single action or, on a Fair (5) *speed load* roll, reloads all six bullets at once. The design isn't quite perfect; the carbine has a Reliability of 19. On a failed check, the weapon jams, requiring a Fair (5) *tinkerin'* or *trade: gunsmith* roll to fix.

Spiller & Burns Tornado. Similar to the Revloving Carbine, this little revolver has break-open breech,

allowing faster reloads. Anyone can load three rounds in an action, while a Fair (5) *speed load* loads all six. The latch is recessed, unlike the S&W Schofield, so there's no risk of looking like a greenhorn when slapping leather with the Tornado!

Tyler Alamo. This is a standard six-shooter with no frills, but nothing fancy to fall apart either. It has a reputation as very reliable and can share ammunition with the Tyler Texan rifle.

Tyler Texan. This high-capacity repeating rifle is especially popular with Confederate cavalry in the West, Texas Rangers, and most other frontiersmen. It's one drawback is that its tubular magazine must be loaded from the muzzle end, instead of the action like a Winchester. This means it takes an additional two actions to reload the Texan in combat.

Whitworth Rifle. This extremely accurate British import is used by Confederate snipers. It's often used in conjunction with a telescopic sight.

ACCORDING TO HOYLE...

FREQUENTLY ASKED QUESTIONS AND CLARIFICATIONS

Welcome to our first installment of *According to Hoyle*. Here, our brand managers will answer some of the most common questions we're asked about our games.

Q: (Wasted West) It says in *Spirit Warriors* that a toxic shaman needs to draw a card each time he invokes a favor. Does he draw from the central Action Deck used by all the other players or does he need his own deck to draw from?

A: The shaman should have his own deck to draw from—otherwise he could wait until both Jokers have been drawn and invoke favors without any risk whatsoever.

Q: (Wasted West) In the Major Mutation Chart in *Children o' the Atom* there is no mutation listed for the 10 of Clubs. What's up with that?

A: That was a mix up at our end. Just to make the chart complete, here's a new mutation to fill in the hole:

10 of Clubs: Your brainer is attuned to dealers of death. By making a Fair (5) *Spirit* roll, your hero can see the auras of those who have taken human life. This ability can be used once per day and lasts for five minutes. Someone who has never killed has no aura, while a person who killed a few people in self-defense might have a grayish glow.

A waster who has killed scores of people has a dark black aura. Note that this doesn't necessarily imply an evil nature—a Templar who has killed hordes of Black Hats would glow just as darkly as a marauder who has slaughtered innocent townspeople.

Q: (Wasted West) The *telekinesis* power says that a syker can lift an amount as if his *Knowledge* were *Strength*, getting a +2 to the die type for each raise on his *blastin'* roll. How do you figure *Strength* for a syker with a 5d12 *blastin'* who gets a few raises?

A: Each raise above a d12 adds +2 to the die type. When calculating the amount lifted, just add the total bonus to 12. A syker who got a result of d12+4 for instance, would have an effective Strength of 16, and could lift 320 pounds according to the Load Table.

Q: (General) Since we're talking about weight, the maximum weights listed on the Load Table seem sort of low. Can't a hero lift any more than that?

As far as the weights listed on the Load Table being too low, the weights on the table were meant to be those that a hero could lift and move around with for an extended period of time. Maximum weights a hero can lift would be closer to Strength X 35. While carrying such weights, the hero has a Pace of 2 and takes 1d4 Wind per round.

Q: (Wasted West) My Doomsayer wants to use *EMP* on some Black Hats. The Black Hats have chipped brain bombs, chipped assault rifles, and they are riding around in a chipped jeep. Does *EMP* work on them, what's the TN, and do their brains automatically explode?

EMP does work on Combine equipment. If a Combine chip is shorted out by EMP, the attached charge detonates immediately. That means a dead Black Hat, if he's the target!

Throckmorton has taken steps to prevent this, of course, so the chips have some degree of hardening against electromagnetic pulses. The chips in individual soldiers and small arms are considered military computers (TN 11). Combine vehicles and large, crew-served weapons have more shielding, requiring a TN of 13 to short.

Q: *(Wasted West)* My Doomsayer wants to target an enemy who is standing a few feet away from a toxic shaman who has invoked the *immunity: radiation* favor. Can I hit my target with a *nuke*?

A: Yes, the *immunity: radiation* favor only blocks radiation miracles which are cast directly on the shaman. It blocks things like *doom plague*, *atomic blast*, and *the questioning hand*—all of which require a specific target—but not area effect miracles like *nuke*, *ICBM*, and the like.

Q: *(General)* I'm not clear on how shotgun slugs work. Does the -2 for firing one replace the usual +2 for using a shotgun, or does it just cancel it out?

The -2 for firing a slug *replaces* the normal +2 bonus for a shotgun. Instead of a +2 bonus to your hero's *shootin'* roll, you get a -2 penalty when firing a slug.

Q: *(General)* The comic in Epitaph #1 was great, but where can I find the profile on the Blood Oak abomination?

A: Right here:

BLOOD OAK

The Reckoning twisted not only animal life, but plants as well, as the blood oak proves all too well. This abomination is a dense, hardwood tree that is found (for now) in the forests of Wisconsin, Michigan, Minnesota. and Canada. Its seeds spread quickly, though, so soon it may be found across the continent.

The tree shares characteristics of oaks, maples...and vampires. Its bark and leaves resemble those of an oak, but it spreads seeds with whirligigs, not unlike a maple. Those seeds can only take root in a dead (or dying) human being, making blood oaks most common around graveyards and battlefields.

The tree has two distinctive features that instantly reveal its true nature. First, the plant's bark and limbs are covered with huge, sword-like thorns. Second, the blood oak's sap is a thick, viscous red fluid—okay, it's really blood—apparently pumped from the corpse from which its roots feed.

Although they remain rooted to one spot, blood oaks are capable of moving their limbs startlingly fast to snare prey—and not just for trees! A final word of warning: Blood oaks normally grow in groves. Where there's one, there's likely to be a dozen of various ages and sizes!

PROFILE: BLOOD OAK

Corporeal: D:1d4, N:2d6, Q:*, S:*, V:*
Fightin': brawlin' 4d6
Mental: C:1d4, K:1d4, M:2d8, Sm:1d6, Sp:*
Pace: 0
Size: *
Wind: —
Terror: 9 (once recognized)
Special Abilities:

  Growth: A blood oak's power depends greatly on its age. Not only do its Coporeal Traits vary, but its special abilities do as well. Each special ability tells you if it has different levels according to age. Blood oaks grow *very* quickly. Saplings are any growth up to 2 years; adolescents are between 2 and 8 years of age; and Mature blood oaks range from 8 years on.

  Size: *Saplings* (Size 7-12); *Adolescent* (Size 12-16); *Mature* (Size 17-20).

  Traits: Certain Corporeal Traits (marked with an *) are age dependent as shown:
  Sapling: Q:3d8, S:4d10, V:4d8
  Adolescent: Q:3d6, S:5d12+2, V:4d12
  Mature: Q:3d4, S:7d12+10, V:6d12+4

  Armor: 2 *Sapling*; 3 *Adolescent*; 4 *Mature*.

  Damage: Branch swat. *Sapling* (STR+2d6); *Adolescent* (STR+2d8); *Mature* (STR+2d10). Additionally, if the blood oak gets a raise on its *fightin'* roll, it has impaled the victim on a thorn, doing double the normal bonus dice to its *Strength* roll for damage (i.e., 4d6, 4d8, or 4d10).

Description: See above.

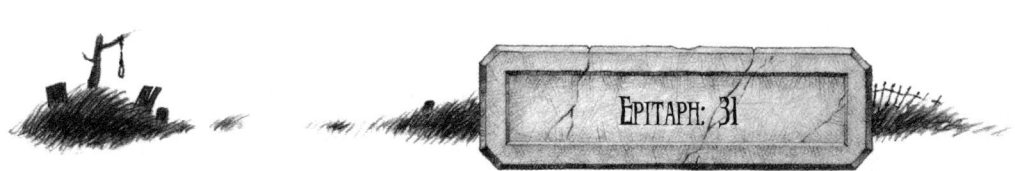

The Medicine Bag:

Junkers

Each installment of *The Medicine Bag* will contain something new in the way of magic for *Deadlands*. This issue we've got a treat for *Hell on Earth's* junkers.

Float

Associated Spirit: Car
TN: 5
Components:
    Chemical: None
    Electronic: 5%
    Mechanical: 15%
    Structural: 10%
Drain: Special/round

Junkers with this power can zip around the Great Maze in style. The *float* power allows techno-shamans to build watercraft of all sorts.

Frame Size

Just like most of the other vehicle powers, you need to select a Frame size for your boat when you begin. This is because many of its components are calculated from the Frame's total slots. Also like the other vehicle powers, you can add passengers, cargo space, weapons, and special equipment as described in the *locomotion* power in *The Junkman Cometh*.

The Engine

The heart of the boat is its engine. Without it, it's just a fancy raft. Your junker has a choice: props or jet.

A propeller system requires a number of slots equal to 5% of the Frame's total slots for each 5 mph of Acceleration desired. The maximum Acceleration rating for a boat is 20 mph.

Putting a jet engine in your ship turns it into a waterborne rocket sled—kind of dangerous in the Maze's twisting canyons, but, hey, it's your hero's funeral. A jet system takes up 10% of the boat's slots for each 5 mph of Acceleration, but a maximum Acceleration of 30 mph is possible.

Top speed for a propeller-driven boat is equal to twice its Frame size plus its Acceleration rating. Top speed for a jet boat is equal to twice its Frame size plus twice its Acceleration. In either case, remember to always round to the nearest 5 mph.

Drain

The Drain for your vessel varies with its drive type.

A prop-driven boat has a Drain equal to its Frame size divided by 3. A jet boat has a Drain equal to its Frame size divided by 2.

If your craft uses spook juice for fuel, prop boats get (20 - Frame) x 3 miles to the gallon, while jet boats get (20 - Frame) x 2 miles per gallon.

Pumps

One thing a boat shouldn't be without is a good set of pumps. (No, not black leather, the kind that pump water.) Of course, pumps are optional, but unless you plan on carrying a lot of buckets to bail with, they're a good idea.

Adding a basic set of pumps takes up 2% of the boat's slots and grants a basic pump rating of 1d4 and increases Drain by 1. Each additional 2% of the ship's slots devoted to pumps increases the pumps' die rating by 1 level (maximum of d8).

It takes one action to turn the pumps on or off. While on, roll the pumps' die each round and subtract this from any flooding damage suffered.

Hydrofoils

If your junker wants to get fancy, she can add some hydrofoils to her creation. These are hydrodynamically shaped lift surfaces mounted at the end of long struts extending down into the water from the hull of the ship—basically they're giant "water wings."

Once the ship reaches a certain speed, the foils generate enough lift to actually raise the hull of the ship up out of the water. This helps in two ways. First, raising the hull out of the water reduces the drag on the boat and allows it to move much faster. It also permits the vessel to move through water that would otherwise be too shallow for it to pass through without running aground.

Adding a set of retractable hydrofoils to a boat takes up 10% of the ship's slots and increases the structural component cost by +5%. It takes an action to activate the deployment or retraction of the foils, and it takes a full round for the foils to lock into place.

Once the foils are deployed, the boat gains their benefits as long as it is moving at least a quarter of its normal Top Speed. While the foils are in use, however, the boat's Top Speed is increased by 50% and it gains a +1 bonus to its Handling.

Using hydrofoils in rough water can be dangerous. Whenever the foils are deployed in Stormy or Hurricane conditions (see *Shattered Coast*), roll 1d20

each round (or every 30 minutes outside combat). If the roll is a 20, one of the hydrofoil struts has snapped under the strain. The driver must make an immediate Incredible (11) *sailin'* roll to keep the craft under control

Submersibles

Your junker can also build a yellow (or green, or whatever) submarine.

Making a boat submersible takes up 30% of its slots right from the start. These slots include ballast tanks, hatches, and a basic periscope.

Subs have one big drawback: They can't be powered by spook juice while submerged. This means that your brainer needs to build in some large batteries or he needs to buddy up with a cyborg that owns a powerjack—otherwise, he's not going anywhere. Your techno-shaman can get around this by adding a snorkel for the engine (5% of the Frame's slots), but this only allows the engine to be used at periscope depth or less (it also leaves a visible wake on the surface).

The ship's Acceleration and Top Speed are halved while submerged beneath the water.

Finishing Touches

Let's figure out the remaining statistics of your personal yacht:

Handling is found by subtracting the vehicle's Frame size from 8 and then adding +1 for each 5 mph of Acceleration rating (maximum of +6, minimum of –4).

Durability is figured as normal for the vehicle's Frame Size.

The boat's Load Limit is equal to 20% of the Frame's total slots.

Each raise on the construction roll can be used to increase Handling by +1, increase the Load Limit by 25%, or increase the top speed by 5 mph.

You're on your own for paint and interior options, though!

A Little Knowledge...

Even as he mounted up in front of the dispatch office, Ronan was amazed that he'd received the telegram at all.

The telegraph was a spotty mode of communication at best, and the fact that not only had it gone through reasonably clear, but Washington had actually sent one to a settlement Ronan had visited was nothing sort of miraculous. Those two occurrences were so rare nowadays that—if Ronan were a religious man—he'd think there was a Higher Power at work.

Thing was, he wasn't.

Still, the wording seemed to indicate his old acquaintance had something of substance to pass along. The telegram read:

Urgent Stop Meet me at the Lazy Horse Hotel in Buckskin Junction Wyoming Territory Stop Will await your arrival for two weeks Stop Life-or-death discovery Stop Twelve purple monkeys Stop Thaddeus Washington Stop

Ronan was fairly certain the last bit— the line about purple monkeys—was a result of either human or mechanical error on the part of the dispatch office. Still, from what he remembered of Thaddeus Washington, the chance his news somehow involved a pack of brightly colored baboons couldn't be completely ruled out.

The first and only time he'd met Washington was in a town in Kansas called Varley Flats. He and Washington, along with Texas Ranger Hank Ketchum, had run into a train full of vampires. Washington, a scientist from back East who gave new meaning to the term "greenhorn," insisted on referring to them as "nosferatu."

"Vampire" worked just fine for Ronan.

The man had proved reliable enough back in Kansas, and his advice on the vampires had been square. Ronan figured he owed the man a little consideration for that, so, when Washington said "life or death," Ronan figured he could spare a few days to look in on the man.

* * *

Buckskin Junction was another ghost town in-training. He guessed the little community had hoped to be the next Cheyenne—or even Fort Bridger—but, odds were it was going to be nothing but empty buildings before the end of the decade.

The railroads had passed it, and the dreams of its citizens, by, missing the community by a dozen miles or more. Just like a limb cut off from the blood supply, Buckskin Junction would wither and die.

Still, Ronan found he was more comfortable in backwater towns of this sort lately. Less people to talk if he had a...problem; less people to recognize him from other places.

Even at a distance, he could tell Buckskin Junction fit the mold perfectly. Not counting a private home or two, there were no more than half-a-dozen buildings in town, and he'd wager at least one or two of those were empty.

Ronan's guess was the town marshal was a part-timer—if Buckskin Junction even had one anymore. A circuit preacher served the spiritual needs of the few left in town, and, in an ironic twist on the old money lenders in the temple story, probably in the saloon on Sunday afternoons. Assuming the founders had lured a newspaper here in the first place, the editor had long packed up his hand press, leaving no one to write Buckskin Junction's obituary when the time came.

While much of that was purely supposition, Ronan figured he was pretty close to the mark. You ride into enough of these towns and you get an eye for them. He saw one thing was for certain: finding the Lazy Horse Hotel wasn't going to be tough. It was the only hotel in town.

Parked in front of it, half-mired in the Wyoming mud pit that passed for the town's only street, was Washington's steam wagon, puffing out steam like an adolescent locomotive. Sitting on the driver's bench adjusting controls and pulling levers was Thaddeus Washington.

* * *

"Mr. Lynch, it certainly is a pleasure to see you," Washington said as the men took a table in the Lazy Horse's saloon. "I'd just about given up hope on you responding to my query."

"Well, you're lucky your telegram reached me at all," Ronan poured himself a whiskey from the bottle he'd secured at the bar. Washington had declined to join him, so the gunslinger figured he'd better get started early if he was going to empty the whole thing a shot glass at a time. "How'd you know where to find me, anyway?"

"Oh, I didn't. I simply eliminated where I knew you weren't, then, based on your observed behaviors, I postulated areas you'd be likely to frequent, and further narrowed my search by eliminating those I couldn't reach via the telegraph."

"And somehow from all that you figured I'd be in Lake City, Colorado?" Even considering all the unsettling things Ronan had experienced over the past couple of years, he found Washington's explanation a stretch.

"Not at all. I narrowed it down to approximately 328 localities close enough to reach Buckskin Junction within the established time frame. I simply sent a telegram to each. Quite costly, but I suspect I'll be losing my research grant soon anyway."

At that moment, Ronan realized that, no matter how long the scientist spent in the West, Washington would likely always be a greenhorn.

"So, what's this 'life-or-death' business you mentioned?" As an afterthought, he added, "And do purple monkeys have anything to do with it?"

"Monkeys? No—I must say Mr. Lynch, that's an odd question. As to the rest, that's a bit of a long story, but I'll make it as brief as possible; I fear time may be short."

KNOWLEDGE...

* * *

"As you may remember, I came West to study emergent species and unique specimens of zoology. Of particular interest to me were the so-called 'Mojave rattlers' found in and around the Great Salt Lake region of Deseret—pardon me, Utah. I've spent over a year there and I'm afraid I've picked up some of the vernacular."

"Yeah," Ronan replied, "I remember you mentioning those worms. In fact, had a run-in with them myself. Me and old One-Eye Ketchum. You remember him?"

"Yes. And in light of recent events, perhaps none to fondly. You see I was successful in much of my research. I discovered a startling number of creatures not cataloged during the course of my field work. Creatures that, given their proximity to mankind, should very well have been. I attempted first to report these findings to my former colleagues, but was mocked. Next, I approached a European organization calling itself the "Explorer's Society."

"They were quite receptive to my studies and expressed interest in publishing my work," Thaddeus continued. "Unfortunately, Captain Ketchum—or one of his comrades-in-arms—intercepted and confiscated my packet of documents. I received notice from Captain Ketchum himself that such endeavors were considered likely to spread panic among the populace of the Confederacy and therefore criminally negligent."

"Of course, his language was much more colorful and...picturesque."

"I'm sure it was," Ronan said. "So what's the point? You've got your dander up over One-Eye?"

"While my 'dander' is indeed 'up,' Mr. Lynch, I've come to expect such short-sighted behavior from the authorities, academic or governmental. No, what I contacted you regarding is far more serious."

"During my visit to Salt Lake City, I met a man by the name of R. Percy Sitgreaves. A most enlightened individual, both in the sciences and more esoteric studies. He revealed to me matters of shocking import to not only my research, but to the future of mankind as a whole."

"You see, Mr. Sitgreaves is an inventor, not unlike myself. However, he is also an occultist. Until recently, I believed such was nothing but the result of glib speech and nimble fingers. I know longer hold that hypothesis."

"Mr. Sitgreaves has shown me convincing evidence that the origin of the unusual advances in technology are related to the same strange evolution I have been chronicling in the natural world. And, in light of his supporting documentation and demonstrations, the only conclusion I can logically deduce is that humanity is being manipulated by an otherworldly source."

Ronan remained silent. Another man might have laughed out loud at the bespectacled scientist, but then again, that man probably didn't have to fight a constant battle for control of his own body with a squirming demon hiding in his head. The gunslinger had suspected since he clawed his way out of his own grave that something was rotten in the world.

"I've devoted the last year to collating data and compiling documents to prove Sitgreaves' theories. The evidence is incontrovertible: On or about July 3, 1863, the laws of Nature as we understand them, changed in a subtle—and dare I say sinister—fashion. Mr. Lynch, somewhere outside of our normal perceptions a dark force is apparently manipulating the future of humanity. To what end, I've yet to determine, but the facts are undeniable."

"Okay, Washington," Lynch said. "What am I supposed to do? I'm a gunfighter, not a witch."

"So, you accept my statements as fact?" Thaddeus seemed truly surprised—even shocked—that Ronan hadn't laughed him out of the saloon.

"Fact? Maybe not, but for reasons of my own, I'll give you the benefit of the doubt—for now."

"I must admit that's a relief. I suspected you might be receptive to my theory in light of our experiences in the vicinity of Varney Flats, but one can never be certain..."

"Okay, so you still haven't told me what you want from me. A testimonial? Somehow I doubt that'll carry much weight."

"No, Mr. Lynch," Thaddeus answered as he rose from his chair. "What I need from you is your talent with your revolver. I've been around the West enough to realize that you're good— perhaps among the best. I'd like to hire you as a bodyguard for the next few weeks."

"Bodyguard?" Ronan squinted at Thaddeus. "If you think my six-gun is going to stop whatever it is behind this conspiracy of yours, then it can't be all that supernatural."

"Not from the authors of humanity's peril, Mr. Lynch, but from those who would keep it secret. You see, in his message, Capt. Ketchum also warned me of organizations on both sides of the law that wished to keep a lid on certain occurrences. Out of respect for our former association, he cautioned me against further investigation on peril of my own life."

"Yeah, that old wolf's a real compassionate man—for a vicious bastard."

"Events of the past couple of months have convinced me of the veracity of his warning. I've been able to keep ahead of my pursuers to date, but I doubt I can for much longer. I need your skill with your 'six-gun' to hold them at bay long enough for me to pass my documents along to someone who can guarantee some measure of protection."

"And who would that be?" Ronan asked.

"Why the fifth estate, Mr. Lynch—the press! To be specific, the *Tombstone Epitaph*. Once my findings are made public, there is no logical reason for any organization to seek my demise."

"Logic never stopped a bullet, Washington."

"Nonetheless, I'm prepared to offer you $10 a day to safeguard me to Tombstone. As I said, I can afford to be generous with what grant money remains to me."

Ronan didn't have to check his pockets to know he was down to his last few dollars. The scientist was offering a generous sum for a baby-sitting job. Besides, figured old Ketchum was probably just trying to put a scare into Washington with rumors of shadowy organizations—other than the Rangers, anyway.

"What the Hell. When do I start?".

* * *

Ronan tossed the last of Thaddeus' baggage aboard the steam wagon. He could have sworn he'd signed on to pack a gun, not luggage. The scientist finished twisting a few knobs and checking a dial or two and then hopped down from the wagon.

"That appears be nearly all of my equipment, Mr. Lynch," he said. "If you could tie it down in the cargo compartment for me, I'll retrieve the documents from my room and we can be off."

Ronan grumbled none to quietly as he climbed aboard to finish the loading. It was already nearing dusk, but Thaddeus insisted they not spend any longer in Buckskin Junction. "I've been here nearly two weeks already, and I fear every night brings my pursuers closer." Ronan had noted that the scientist never placed a name to his 'pursuers.' The gunman had heard tell of inventors who weren't quite in touch with reality, and he was starting to suspect his companion's paranoia might be the beginnings of full-blown madness.

"Oh, and Mr. Lynch—be careful to not engage that lever to your left," Thaddeus called from the hotel door just a moment before Ronan was going to push the very one forward. "That will seal the stack to build up an overpressurization; if the powertrain is not engaged within 30 seconds, the pressure chamber will explode!"

Ronan just frowned and squinted at the hotel door. Thaddeus had already stepped inside. Ten dollars a day might not be enough, he thought.

* * *

Nearly half an hour later, Ronan decided he'd best check on the scientist. As soon as he walked through the doors to the hotel's first floor saloon, he knew Thaddeus Washington hadn't been off his rocker.

Three men, all dressed in long black dusters and impeccably clean clothing waited in the drinking establishment, positioned strategically around the room. Ronan had seen enough fights to know an ambush when he saw one.

The bartender's worried expression said he was expecting all Hell to break loose any minute. And, from the way the men turned to face him as he entered, Ronan guessed he was holding the keys to the infernal gates.

"Evenin'," he muttered as he moved to the bar. The men were spread out, covering the front and back door to the room and the stairs leading up to the hotel's private rooms. Ronan walked toward the stairs, trying his best to appear nonthreatening. It wouldn't serve his best interests to have guns clear leather in here.

At least not until he was ready.

When he reached the bottom of the stairs, the man positioned there rose from his chair and put an arm across the bannister, blocking the gunslinger's way.

"'Scuse me, friend," the man said. "Where you headed?"

"To my room," Ronan growled. "Who's asking?"

"Isaiah Trent," the man in the duster replied. "I'm here on behalf of the United States Government to assist in the apprehension of Confederate spy Thaddeus Washington and his accomplices, if any. You wouldn't happen to know the man would you? Don't bother answering—we've been watching you load his steam wagon for the past half-hour."

"Why don't you draw your gun out real careful like with two fingers on your left hand and put it on the table over there?" Trent continued.

"And here I thought we were friends," Ronan said. Following the man's instructions, he slowly pulled his six-shooter and laid it on the table. "Now that's out of the way, mind telling me why you're really here? Only a blind idiot would try to claim Washington was a Confederate agent. While I can't attest to the second part of that ,I know you're not blind."

Trent's eyes narrowed but he didn't answer immediately. Instead, he motioned to the man closest to the front door, and the gunman slipped out the front. Then, drawing a bulky, odd-looking, multi-barreled pistol, he waved the barkeep out of the room. He took a seat and indicated to Ronan to do the same.

"This is downright cozy," Ronan commented. "If we had some candles and a nice meal, I'd think you was courtin' me, mister."

"Cute—Lynch, is it?" the man answered. From his accent, Ronan placed him back East, maybe New England. "What has Washington told you?"

"Let's see, I got a telegram talking about purple apes or something like that. I'd show it to you, but you've got me so nervous I don't think my fingers would work right. Besides, I'd hate for your friend over there see me stick my hand in my pocket and get antsy—especially if he's totin' a Gatling pistol too."

Deliberately and slowly, the gunslinger pulled the flap of his jacket open. Trent reached across for the pocket, keeping his gun point in Ronan's direction.

At just that moment a staccato burst of gunfire sounded from outside, followed immediately by two distinctly different shots.

* * *

Trent, momentarily distracted, turned toward the sound of the gunshots. Seizing the opportunity, Ronan grabbed his hand, leaned back in his chair, and kicked the table toward the man's legs. His weight pulled his captor toward him as the table took his feet out from under him.

Ronan's chair reared back and fell, dropping both men to the ground. The gunslinger made sure his knee caught Trent solid in the gut when he landed, knocking the wind out of him and sending his fancy clockwork pistol skittering across the floor away from both men's reach. The impact left Trent momentarily stunned and Ronan rolled out of the tangle of limbs and chair legs.

Only to stand up into a hail of bullets as the other man opened up with his Gatling pistol.

Diving across the table to retrieve his own weapon, Ronan was peppered with wood splinters as the bullets ripped into the table top. He let his momentum carry him across the table and back to the floor on the other side.

Ronan couldn't risk standing up to get a good shot at the man and the intervening table and chairs prevented him from taking the gunman out with a shot to the legs. Trent was groaning behind him and starting to get his bearings back. If the gunslinger didn't act fast, he'd be caught between the two.

Watching the man's legs move along the back wall, Ronan tracked him through the room. As he crossed under one of the saloon's wall lamps, Ronan fanned two rounds into the glass globe. The oil splashed across the man's back and flared as the burning wick landed on him, setting his long duster ablaze.

While he thrashed and flailed to remove his burning coat, the gunslinger rose and spun to face Trent, also back on his feet. His Gatling pistol was a good six feet away, so Ronan just shook his head and motioned for him to step away.

Suddenly, Trent's hand flicked and a derringer sprung into his palm. Ronan with supernatural quickness put two rounds solidly into the man's chest sending him stumbling backward into another table.

In moments, it was over. Both of his opponents lay dead or at least out of action. All things considered, it could have been much worse, he thought.

Then he heard the deliberate and hollow echo of boots on wood and the creak of the saloon door behind him.

* * *

Framed in the doorway and silhouetted by the last light of the dying day stood a man in a long coat. The coat was old—so old, in fact, that Ronan couldn't be certain, but he thought it might have once been part of a Confederate sergeant's uniform. The years had turned it a dark brown.

Light glinted of what appeared to be medals or maybe badges on the lower left corner of the coat's flaps and a single feather adorned the man's tattered hat. In his right hand he held an old Army revolver, its barrel still smoking. Ronan could see the bulge of a second pistol under his worn coat.

The man said nothing as he slowly surveyed the room. It was then Ronan noticed his left hand was covered in blood so thick that it dripped onto the saloon floor. He could almost hear the splashes of each swollen drop.

Ronan's brow creased, but he only stared silently at the man when the stranger's gaze reached him.

"You must be Lynch," the dark man said in a voice stolen from a dried-up desert grave. "I wasn't looking for you…yet. But now's as good a time as any."

"Why?" Ronan grated. "You got your tombstone already picked out?"

"You got grit, Lynch—I'll give you that. But unless I missed my count, you've only got two bullets left to back it up. And, I didn't miss my count."

"Mister, the only bullet of mine you need to worry about is the one with your name on it. And, since I doubt either of us wants me to take the time to pull it out and read it, why don't you tell me who the Hell you are. And why I should care."

"The name's Stone," the stranger answered. "As to why you should care…"

A series of three sharp gunshots sounded from Ronan's right and he saw the stranger's tattered coat pick up a couple of newer holes.

40   KNOWLEDGE…

Ronan turned to see the man he'd set afire standing near the wall a little singed, but otherwise none the worse for wear.

"That'll be enough, Lynch," he heard Trent's voice say. Glancing over his shoulder, he saw the man standing apparently uninjured, although he could clearly see the holes in the man's coat where his own bullets had struck home. The man had retrieved his pistol and had it leveled at the gunslinger.

"Doesn't anyone stay dead anymore?" he growled.

"Unfortunately, no," Trent answered. "Now put your pistol back down and you may still walk out of here. Like the man said, you've only got two bullets—one, if you're an old-timer that only loads five— and that's not enough to settle with us."

"You didn't kill him, Lynch," the stranger's grating voice crawled from the doorway. "He and his partners are wearing bulletproof vests. That's why it took me two shots to kill the first one."

Trent seemed a little surprised to see the man still standing, but not overly so. "Okay, mister. You're interfering with U.S. Government affairs here. On behalf of the U.S. Special Services Agency, I order you to drop your weapons or we'll put you in a pine box."

"I figured you was Agency. There's too many of you to be Rangers," the man said. "I'll make you fellows a deal, then. You tell me where to find Washington and I'll make sure you die quick."

Damn, Ronan thought. If the Agency and the goon in the door really were after him, maybe Thaddeus Washington had been right all along.

"He's long gone, mister. We've already collected him," Trent answered, his eyes on the man in the door. "We were just finishing up with Lynch, so you ease those pistols onto the floor."

"Well, then, if he's gone, I reckon I got no need of you folks, then do I?" With that, he hipshot the second agent in the gun arm while drawing his second pistol and firing twice at Trent before even Ronan could react.

Ronan caught a flash of light from Trent's hand and a fan of poker cards appeared there. The gunslinger had seen enough of Velvet Van Helter's tricks to know Trent was slinging a hex.

Deftly Trent flicked two cards into the air and Ronan saw them jerk sharply and drop to the floor. When they hit, he noticed each had a deformed lump of lead stuck to it—bullets.

The stranger seemed unconcerned and strode over to the wounded agent who was still stunned from his injury. The man holstered one of his pistols and grabbed the agent by the throat, pulling him up to eye level. Then he opened his mouth unnaturally wide and the gunslinger could have sworn he saw the man's breath literally being drawn from his body.

In mere moments, the man was a drawn and wasted shadow of his former self. The stranger dropped the body and turned toward Ronan and Trent. In the better light, Ronan could tell the man's skin was drawn and decaying. Like the gunslinger, the stranger was no longer living, but animated by an unholy force within his body, although his physical body showed the signs of death that, as yet, Ronan's did not.

Trent's hands produced another set of cards and a ghostly white stream streaked from him toward the man. It struck his chest with an audible thump, but the man only huffed a little and then smiled at the pair.

"You'll have to do much better than that," he said. "And I don't think you've got it in you, Agency-man."

Ronan began circling to the right, toward the rear of the saloon, hoping to flank the stranger. The gunslinger sensed this man was possibly the most dangerous adversary he'd ever faced. Or ever would.

The man's gun roared at the agent, but he flicked another card into the air. This time, it failed to completely stop the stranger's bullet and Trent staggered back, blood leaking from a wound in his leg. He fanned his cards again, but this time, instead of energy streaking toward the stranger, it poured up his arm and coursed over his own body.

Trent convulsed as faint white streams surged over his body and then fell motionless to the floor.

"I got friends on the Other Side, Agency-man and they look out for me. Shame you didn't know that before you started playin' your parlor games." The man strode over to the fallen agent his gun drawn for the killing shot, blatantly ignoring Ronan.

"Hey!" the gunslinger yelled. "I think you forgot about me."

* * *

"Not at all, Lynch," the man said. "I was just givin' you some time to think about the future. See, you got two choices."

"What do you mean?" Ronan asked. He doubted he could do much against the stranger with just two bullets, but maybe, if he could keep the man talking, maybe Trent would recover. The agent seemed to have a number of cards up his sleeve; he might have an ace up there as well.

"First choice you got is you can join up with me. We ain't all that different, you and me. Both of us know what the inside of a grave looks like. Wouldn't it be easier to just stop fighin' the voice in your head? After all, it gave you a second chance at life."

Ronan thought about the things the voice whispered to him, the nightmares those words caused. He thought about what feeling his own flesh rot was like, about how having an empty, numb shell for a body felt. The thing that brought him back was no friend; torturer was a better word. Sometimes, he thought, dead was better.

"What's the other choice?"

"The second choice is I put you down for good," the man said in a flat voice. "Not a threat, not a promise, just a fact. I do that, though, I kill the thing that's keepin' you alive as well. I don't want to do that, but if a thing's got to be done..."

"You forgot the third choice," Ronan said, a plan finally forming. He hoped the

thing in his head wanted to stay alive as much as he thought it did.

"Oh, this is where you tell me you could kill me, right?" the man said. "You can't take me—we both know that—so don't waste your breath."

"No, you can go to Hell!" Ronan said and snapped off his last two bullets.

They whizzed past the stranger's ear and passed harmlessly through the saloon's front window in a tinkling rain of glass.

"I'm already on my way, but not today and damn sure not by your hand, Lynch. Honestly, I expected better from you after what I'd heard."

"Damn," Ronan said through gritted teeth. "You can't blame a man for tryin'. At least tell me your name. There's nothin' I hate worse than gettin' shot by strangers."

The man actually laughed a little, although it was one of the most unpleasant sounds Ronan could recall.

"Fair enough, Lynch. The name's Stone. When you get to Hell, you tell 'em I sent you." With that, he pulled his big Army six-gun up and took aim at Ronan's head.

A whistle like a giant's tea kettle reaching a boil split the air. Stone whirled to see a valve rocket through the shattered window and bounce off a wall. Ronan grinned like a wolf; at least one of his bullets had hit its target—the overpressure lever on Washington's steam wagon.

"Tell 'em yourself," Ronan said as the engine erupted in white hot fury.

* * *

He wasn't sure if it was hours or minutes later when he pulled himself from under the table he'd dived beneath as the steam wagon exploded. From the looks of it, the gizmo had taken nearly half the front of the hotel with it.

Ronan saw no evidence of Stone anywhere in the rubble. If God looked out for drunkards, fools, and children, apparently the Devil had a few favorites of his own as well. He did find Trent pinned under the ruins of the bar.

Surprisingly, the agent was still breathing, though Ronan guessed it would be a while before he'd be menacing anyone in his long coat again.

KNOWLEDGE...

He slapped the man sharply in the face a couple of times. When that failed to revive him, he dug around until he found a mostly intact whiskey bottle and poured it on him.

Coughing weakly, Trent sputtered awake.

"Trent," Ronan said, looming over the trapped man, "I ain't one to kill a helpless man, but I can be real clumsy. I might accidentally step on a broken bone or two if I were to hang around too long. The best way to get me to move along is to tell me where you had Washington taken."

"Won't...do...you any...good," he coughed.

"You tell me and I'll be the judge of that—or don't tell me and you can be the judge of how much my boot heel hurts on your wrist."

"Denver...but if you go there...you'll be getting more than you bargained for..." With that, the agent passed back into unconsciousness.

"At ten dollars a day, I *already* got more than I bargained for," Ronan said as he stumbled out of the collapsed building. He looked around, hoping his horse had survived the explosion.

Denver was a long walk.

NEW HEX

HOLE CARD

Trait: Knowledge
Hand: Jacks
Speed: 1
Duration: 1 round/*hexslingin'* level

Trick shots like to plug a hole in a playing card to prove their skill, but no one ever plans to face down the Ace of Spade in a gunfight. This hex might leave gunslingers wishing they'd learned how to *miss* the darn things!

Hole card turns the cards conjured up by your huckster into one-shot bullet (or arrow) stoppers. Just like when your huckster slings the hex *cardsharp*, the cards that appear in his hand when the hex is cast remain until used or the duration expires. Instead of deadly missiles, the cards created by *hole card* are tiny shields your magician can flick in the way of incoming attacks.

To use a card to block a missile attack, your cowpoke must make a

vamoose (spend his highest action card). Wait until you see if the attack has hit, but before damage is rolled.

Once you've decided to block an attack, choose one of the cards from the five your character kept for his final hand. Your huckster then flips the magical card into the air where it intercepts the incoming missile—no roll necessary!

The card acts like light armor, and blocks a random amount of damage based on its suit and value. This amount is determined by a dice roll.

The type of dice depends on the chosen card's value, just as it did when you created your character. Deuces are d4s, 3s through 8s are d6s, 9s through Jacks are d8s, Queens and Kings are d10s, and Aces are d12s. Jokers are equal to the value of the card they copy in the final hand.

The number of dice is based on the suit, again, as in character creation. Clubs are one die, Diamonds two, Hearts three, and Spades four.

So, a Nine of Spades, for example, means you roll 4d8. Add up the dice and subtract the total from the damage from the missile. If the hit location is the noggin or gizzards, the bonus dice are added to the damage roll *before* the hex's total is subtracted.

Any damage left over hits your hero in the location indicated.

Once a card is used, it's gone; each card blocks a single attack. Against attacks that generate multiple missiles on a single action, like fanning, *shard*, or Gatling guns, your huckster can throw one card for each missile.

Hole card works against all forms of missile attacks, whether physical (thrown knives, arrows, bullets, even cannon balls) or magical (*soul blast*, *bolts o' doom*, etc.).

The hex is useless against hand-to-hand attacks., nor does it work against area of effect weapons, such as flamethrowers, *soul burst*, *sliver spray*, and other explosions.

VARMINTS!:
SPIRITS & SHIPS

We've rustled up a couple of new abominations to plague your posse. The first is reported by a ferner from someplace called "New Zealand," and, trust us, it's sure to give the most hardened cowpokes a ride for their money. The other is horror straight from the Davey Jones' Locker.

SPIRIT 'GLOM
BY BRIAN LEYBOURNE

A spirit 'glom is a similar entity to a 'glom or a bone 'glom, but is a fusing of the angry spirits of the dead, rather than their bodies or bones. Like other 'gloms, spirit 'glom's are only created in areas where mass killings have taken place, such as old battlefields.

The spirit 'glom needs a focus—a physical body. Usually, the focus body is that of an officer, leader, or other powerful person slain at the site. This body houses the essence of all the spirits in the spirit 'glom, preventing them from reaching their rightful place in the afterlife. This even hinders their return as Harrowed. The more spirits fused into a spirit 'glom, the more powerful it is.

During the initial creation of a spirit 'glom, it only fuses the most powerful spirits of the recently dead, so that even in a battle where nearly 1000 men died, perhaps only 10 or 20 spirits might be fused into the spirit 'glom. Later, when the spirit 'glom adds spirits to itself, it can take any spirit regardless of its power.

Generally, the entity is confined to the area of the battle that formed it. At night, the spirit 'glom appears as rolling mist, covering the battlefield where the massacre took place. The more spirits fused in the spirit 'glom, the larger the area of mist. The spirit 'glom has control over the physical form of the mist, such that it can form solid tendrils of mist, and use these to strike out at anyone within or near the body of mist.

The spirit 'glom is capable of animating the bodies of the spirits contained within it, and these *may* travel up to two miles outside the mist. These are under the full control of the spirit 'glom, but should in all other ways be treated as walkin' dead with the same statistics including their resistance to damage other than to the head. Marshal, you may choose to make them veteran walkin' dead; the victims are most often soldiers, after all!

Anyone killed inside the 'glom's mist itself, either by one of the zombies or by the spirit 'glom's tendrils, is added to the abomination, making it more powerful, as well as providing another body for it to animate.

This makes it unlikely the victim can come back Harrowed. Marshal, make the normal Harrowed pull but with three less cards than normal. If the character pulls no Joker, she's now part of the spirit 'glom.

If the spirit 'glom can raise the fear level of an area to five or above, then any person killed by one of the monster's walkin' dead rises as another zombie, even if she was not within the mist at the time. Generally, the spirit 'glom will cause the bodies it has animated to dig themselves into the ground during the day to remain hidden.

PROFILE: SPIRIT 'GLOM (FOCUS BODY)

Corporeal: D:2d8, N:2d8, Q: 2d12, S:1d10, V:2d8

Dodge 2d8, fightin': brawlin' 3d8

Mental: C:1d10*, K:1d6, M:1d10*, Sm:1d6, Sp:1d12*

Overawe 5d10, tendril lash: 3d12

Pace: 8 (Focus Body only)

Size: 6 (Focus Body; Mist size may cover entire battlefield)

Wind: NA

Terror: 11

Special Abilities:

Damage: Bite: (STR)

Immunity: Physical and magical damage. The mist form of the spirit 'glom is incorporeal and can't be harmed by any means.

Tendril Lash: Misty Tendrils. The spirit 'glom can make one tendril attack per action for every three

spirits it has fused into itself, but never more than one attack per opponent in the mist. It uses its *tendril lash* Aptitude, which is based on *Spirit*, due to the nature of the tendril, to do so. This attack ignores inanimate objects (like armor), but it may be *dodged*. It does damage based on *Spirit*, not *Strength*. The spirit 'glom may also make a bite attack with its focus (physical) body on the same action.

Undead: Focus—Focus Body. The only way to destroy a spirit 'glom is to destroy its focus body, which is generally difficult as the creature is likely to keep that body safely hidden under the ground most of the time. To absorb the spirits of freshly killed people, however, it is necessary for the focus body of the spirit 'glom to be in the exact center of the mist, so the best time to kill one is to catch it while it is absorbing spirits. To add to the fun, this body is extremely resistant to damage from any source that is not consecrated by the *consecrate armament* miracle, making it difficult to kill without the aid of one of the Blessed. *Consecrated* weapons or bullets do normal damage to the prime body of the spirit 'glom, but all damage from other sources is divided by 5 before it is applied (this includes magical attacks like *soul blast*). Additionally, only a Maiming wound to the head can kill the focus body. Other wounds are regenerated at a rate of one wound level per round (total, not per hit location).

Description: Spirit 'gloms are normally only encountered after dark. It appears as a large area of mist — sometimes hundreds of yards across. The focus body when above ground appears as a normal walkin' dead, except the mist extrudes from its body–particularly the mouth and any death wounds.

LEGENDARY HORROR

Here's an abomination from the legends of the sea that didn't make it into *RVC II: The Book of Curses*. Since we can't keep an evil ship's captain down—and apparently, neither can the sea!—we thought we'd throw him out for you to haunt the shores of your campaign.

THE FLYING DUTCHMAN

During the 16th century, a sailing vessel by the name of *The Flying Dutchman* was carrying a fortune in gold and goods. Its captain, a man named Vanderdecken, decided to kill the owner of the cargo, cast his body overboard, and claim the treasure for himself. Promising his crew a share of the treasure, Vanderdecken set a course around the Cape of Good Hope.

Soon the vessel was beset by a plague that claimed the lives of all aboard except the captain and his cabin boy. As *The Flying Dutchman* entered the treacherous straits, a ferocious storm whipped up. In a drunken rage, Vanderdecken dared the Almighty himself to sink his vessel and fired his pistol toward Heaven.

Instead of being dashed against the rocks, Vanderdecken was cursed with a worse fate. He now sails the the world's oceans forever, plaguing other sailors. Only his cabin boy—now a demonic imp—remains, although he can call forth the dead of the sea to do his bidding.

Vanderdecken and his ghostly vessel may be encountered in lonely stretches of water along the lonely northeastern shores of the U.S., the Gulf Coast or in the haunted channels of the Maze. He usually tries to chase or force vessels—particularly those carrying valuable cargoes—into hazardous waters.

On rare occasions, he may even pull *The Flying Dutchman* alongside a ship and board it with a crew of undead.

GHOST SHIP

The Flying Dutchman is a floating haunted house. It raises the Fear Level on any vessel that sights it by 2 and has a constant Fear Level 5 itself.

The ship can keep pace with the fastest vessels on the water. Because it is powered by its master's curse, it can maintain its speed even in dead calm, it's sails billowing with ghostly winds. The vessel is immune to all normal damage and any dealt from a magical source is repaired the next time the ghost ship appears.

The vessel can change its appearance to deceive other vessels. It's been described as a four-master, a schooner, or a brig. Sailors claim to have seen the ship glow red with the blood of its victims or even sail beneath the sea.

On occasions, Vanderdecken may dispatch a rowboat from *The Flying Dutchman*. Although the boat is apparently empty, it somehow overtakes other vessels, as if to moor with them. If it manages to pull alongside, everyone on board is saddled with the *bad luck* Hindrance until the ship reaches its port.

PROFILE: CAPTAIN VANDERDECKEN

Corporeal: D:3d8, N:2d8, Q:3d6, S:4d8, V:2d10

Climbin' 3d8, fightin': brawlin', knife 4d8, shootin': pistol 7d8

Mental: C:3d12, K:2d6, M:2d10, Sm:3d8, Sp:1d10

Area knowledge: oceans 6d6, overawe 4d10, ridicule 4d8, trade: seaman 7d6, search 5d12, scrutinize 3d12

Pace: 8

Size: 6

Wind: 20

Terror: 9

Special Abilities:

Coup: A Harrowed counting coup on Vanderdecken becomes an uncanny shot with a pistol (and only a pistol). As long as he spends at least one Action Card drawing a bead, he *cannot* miss a target (or hit location) as long as it is within his pistol's first range increment.

Damage: Pistol (3d8). Vanderdecken's old flintlock pistol has a ROF 1 and reloads after every shot.

The Flying Dutchman: *The Flying Dutchman* can ignore any rules on movement. It can stop in a single action and perform maneuvers impossible to a normal vessel. It can also submerge itself—although this is likely to appear to onlookers as though it is sinking. The ship cannot be sunk until Vanderdecken is destroyed himself.

Immunity—Normal Damage: Normal weapons cannot harm Vanderdecken. Even magical weapons, spells, and the like can only temporarily dispatch him. The only ways to destroy the captain are to shoot him with his own pistol or fire a bullet made of gold taken from a sunken treasure ship into his heart (-10 to *shootin'* rolls).

Ship's Master: The sea's full of dead and Vanderdecken can call upon them to serve him. He can summon up to 30 skeletons, bloats, or plain old walkin' dead—depending on what's available in the area (your call, Marshal). These abominations follow his orders faithfully for one 24-hour period. He can use this power once per week.

Description: Vanderdecken looks like a 16th century sea captain in his early '50s. He has a white beard and moustache and always wears his pistol stuck in his belt. His features are sunken and pallid and his eyes are empty black orbs. His deep booming voice has a gurgling quality, as if his throat is clogged with seawater.

PROFILE: THE CABIN BOY

Corporeal: D:3d8, N:3d10, Q:4d10, S:3d8, V:4d12

Climbin' 6d10, dodge 4d10, fightin': brawlin' 5d10, sneak 3d10

Mental: C:3d12, K:2d6, M:3d6, Sm:3d10, Sp:2d12

Overawe 4d6, ridicule 5d10, search 6d12, trade: seaman 5d6

Pace: 10

Size: 5

Wind: 24

Terror: 7

Special Abilities:

Armor: -4 (light).

Damage: Bite (STR+1d4).

Head Butt: If the cabin boy moves his full Pace prior to an attack, he can butt an opponent with his horns with a successful *fightin': brawlin'* attack. This does STR+1d6 brawling damage. With a raise, the attack knocks opponents with Size 6 or less off their feet.

Immunity: The cabin boy takes damage from all attacks—normal and magical—but cannot be destroyed as long as Vanderdecken exists. He appears the next night fully healed.

Description: The cabin boy is a small, demonic creature. He has a pair of horns sprouting from his forehead and his mouth is filled with over-sized and unnaturally sharp teeth. His brownish skin is tough and abrasive to the touch , not unlike that of a shark. Still, in spite of his strange appearance, he retains a few child-like features, which makes the creature even more unsettling.

DEADLANDS PRODUCT LIST

DEADLANDS: THE WEIRD WEST

SKU	Price	Title
1100	25	Player's Guide (hardback)
1101	25	Marshal's Guide (hardback)
1003	20	Book o' the Dead
1004	20	Smith & Robards
1005	20	Hucksters & Hexes
1006	20	Rascals, Varmints, & Critters
1007	4.95	Twisted Tales
1008	30	Great Maze (box)
1009	15	Marshal Law (Screen)
1010	20	Ghost Dancers
1011	20	Fire & Brimstone
1012	30	Fortress o' Fear (box)
1014	30	City o' Gloom (box)
1015	20	Law Dogs
1016	9.95	Road to Hell
1017	9.95	Heart o' Darkness
1018	20	Tales o' Terror 1877
1019	20	Lost Angels
1020	30	River o' Blood (box)
1021	30	Boomtowns (box)
1022	9.95	Marshal's Log
1023	25	Doomtown or Bust
1024	9.95	Bloody Ol' Muddy
1025	20	Back East: North
1026	20	Back East: South
1027	20	South o' the Border
1028	20	Canyon o' Doom (Jan)
1029	20	RVC 2: Book o' Curses
1030	20	The Agency (April)
1031	15	Ghost Busters (April)
1032	20	Hexarcana (June)
1033	20	The Collegium (Aug)
1034	15	Rain o' Terror (Aug)
1035	20	The Great Weird North (Oct)
1036	20	The Black Circle (Dec)
1037	15	Dead Presidents (Dec)

WEIRD WEST CARDSTOCK COWBOYS

SKU	Price	Title
2701	19.95	Weird West Starter Pack
2702	14.95	Horrors
2703	14.95	Infernal Devices (June)
2704	14.95	Doomtown! (Aug)
2705	14.95	Great Rail Wars (Oct)
2706	14.95	Here Comes the Cav! (Dec)

WEIRD WEST DIME NOVELS

SKU	Price	Title
9000	4.95	Perdition's Daughter (OP)
9001	4.95	Independence Day (OP)
9002	4.95	Night Train
9003	4.95	Strange Bedfellows
9004	4.95	Savage Passage
9005	4.95	Ground Zero
9006	4.95	Forbidden God
9007	4.95	Adios Amigos
9008	6.95	Skinners
9009	6.95	Worms!

DEADLANDS: HELL ON EARTH ROLEPLAYING GAME

SKU	Price	Title
6000	30	Hell on Earth (hardback)
6001	15	Radiation Screen
6002	20	Brainburners
6003	20	Children o' the Atom
6004	9.95	Hell or High Water
6005	25	Wasted West
6006	4.95	Toxic Tales
6007	20	Road Warriors
6008	20	The Last Crusaders
6009	20	The Junkman Cometh
6010	9.95	Something About a Sword
6011	20	Monsters, Muties, and Misfits
6012	20	Cyborgs
6013	25	Iron Oasis (Jan)
6014	15	The Boise Horror (Feb)
6015	20	Spirit Warriors (March)
6016	25	Shattered Coast (May)
6017	30	Denver (box) (July)
6018	15	Urban Renewal (July)
6019	20	Waste Warriors (Sept)
6020	20	City o' Sin (Nov)
6021	15	The Unity (Nov)

HELL ON EARTH DIME NOVELS

SKU	Price	Title
9501	4.95	Leftovers
9502	4.95	Infestations
9503	6.95	Killer Klowns

HELL ON EARTH CARDSTOCK COWBOYS

SKU	Price	Title
2801	19.95	Wasted West Starter (Feb)
2802	14.95	Horrors (March)
2803	14.95	Road Wars! (May)
2804	14.95	The Combine (July)
2805	14.95	Muties! (Sept)

YOU CAN ORDER VIA OUR WEBPAGE, WWW.DEADLANDS.COM, OR OUR 800 NUMBER, (800) 214-5645 (ORDERS OLY)

STORY
CLAY AND SUSAN
GRIFFITH

ART
RICHARD POLLARD

COLORS
CHUCK CROFT &
ZEKE SPARKES

LETTERS
CHRIS LIBEY

HELL HOLE

Lost Colony

SHOWDOWN

www.deadlands.com

Fear The Reapers

chapter 1

GURPS DEADLANDS

The Weird West Just Got Weirder!

Steve Jackson Games and Pinnacle are pleased to present *GURPS Deadlands*. With this "crossover" book, Marshals can bring their *Deadlands* heroes into more than 60 settings for *GURPS*, or supplement the terrors of the Weird West with new creatures from *GURPS* books such as *Undead* and *Creatures of the Night*. No matter which game you play, *GURPS Deadlands* will open up new worlds of adventure!

Expand Your Game With GURPS

GURPS, the Generic Universal RolePlaying System, is the most flexible roleplaying system you can use. Supplements covering many genres are already out – and more are coming! It's easy to learn and "Game Master-friendly."

Adventure on the American frontier with *GURPS Old West, Second Edition*. Travel back to a simpler time, when a man wore the law on his hip and owned only what he could defend . . . a time when danger – and opportunity – lurked over every hill. *Old West* has been extensively researched; it's useful for Marshals who want to add historical accuracy to their *Deadlands* games.

Or try something a little wilder! *GURPS Steampunk* combines the mood of cyberpunk with the setting of an alternate Industrial Age, where computers run on steam power, flying ironclads rule the skies, and science is the new frontier.

GURPS Basic Set, Third Edition Revised: Stock #6022, ISBN 1-55634-127-X, $24.95
GURPS Creatures of the Night: Stock #6066, ISBN 1-55634-273-X, $19.95
GURPS Old West, Second Edition: Stock #6044, ISBN 1-55634-439-2, $19.95
GURPS Steampunk: Stock #6098, ISBN 1-55634-419-8, $20.95
GURPS Undead: Stock #6086, ISBN 1-55634-352-3, $19.95

STEVE JACKSON GAMES
www.sjgames.com